The door was unlocked but he hesitated on the threshold. Time was when he would have walked right into Anna's bedroom without a second thought, he reflected. And she into his.

"You can come in, Jack."

She stood on the deck, her hands buried in the pockets of her pale bathrobe. An evening breeze rustled through the trees and lifted a corner of the fine linen, exposing the long length of a butterscotch-smooth thigh to Jack's hungry gaze.

He dragged his eyes away, trying to blank the thought that the robe might be all she wore. She stepped off the deck onto the slate tiles and slid the door closed behind her.

"Your door should be locked." He barely recognized his own voice. He swallowed. "It's not safe to leave it open."

Anna's eyes gleamed with a flash of mischief. She hadn't grown out of that, or out of the dimple in the middle of her left cheek.

"So it seems," she said.

"No. That's not..." She had him tied in knots and he hadn't even touched her, apart from the handshake earlier, when his world had been shaken up and then dropped around him in a shape he didn't recognize.

Dear Reader,

It is said that you may leave Africa, but Africa will never leave you.

Eleven years ago, Anna fled, her dreams of being with Jack crushed. Now she's back with a plan—a plan that will fix the past and allow her to claim the future she wants.

Yet, to her shock, the place of her birth has not loosened its grip on her soul. And Jack, struggling with his own demons, still holds her heart in his hands.

The remote bushland in the northeast of South Africa is one of my favorite places. On a visit a few years ago, as I lay beneath a thatched roof, the nearby roar of a lion and the more distant, haunting laugh of a hyena filled the predawn dark. My lifelong habit of weaving a mental narrative around the day-to-day events of life clicked into action and *Their Wildest Safari Dream* was born.

I'm excited and thrilled to introduce you to Anna and Jack. Will the pain of the past tear them apart or will their love for each other bind them together forever?

I hope you will love their story as much as I do. Thank you for reading it.

Suzanne

Their Wildest Safari Dream

—

Suzanne Merchant

Recycling programs
for this product may
not exist in your area.

ISBN-13: 978-1-335-73695-6

Their Wildest Safari Dream

Copyright © 2022 by Suzanne Merchant

Harlequin Enterprises ULC
22 Adelaide St. West, 41st Floor
Toronto, Ontario M5H 4E3, Canada
www.Harlequin.com

Printed in U.S.A.

Suzanne Merchant was born and raised in South Africa. She and her husband lived and worked in Cape Town, London, Kuwait, Baghdad, Sydney and Dubai before settling in the Sussex countryside. They enjoy visits from their three grown-up children and are kept busy attempting to wrangle two spaniels, a dachshund, a parrot and a large, unruly garden under control.

Their Wildest Safari Dream
is Suzanne Merchant's debut title for Harlequin.

Visit the Author Profile page at Harlequin.com.

For my family

CHAPTER ONE

ELEVEN YEARS AGO she'd begged Jack to marry her, pleaded with him to make *her* the wife his father demanded he find. Until he had a 'half-decent wife', the old man had shouted, any plans Jack had to drag the Themba reserve and its two hundred square miles of African bush into the twenty-first century could go to hell.

'You, Anna?' Jack had raked his fingers through his hair, frustration and temper simmering in his slate-grey eyes. 'Are you insane? You're just a kid.'

His brutal rejection had bewildered and belittled her.

'I'm eighteen, Jack. Officially an adult, and I...'

'And you're going back to England to take your degree. It's what your mother wanted, remember?' He'd turned his back on her and walked away. 'And anyway,' he'd said, over his shoulder, 'I don't want a wife. Not ever.'

Back then, there had been no airstrip on the

dusty, thorn-dry reserve. There had definitely been no such thing as a helicopter transfer from the little airport at Skukuza. It had been a lurching, rough, seven-hour journey to Johannesburg in an ancient Land Rover Defender, and Jack had taken her on it the following day, three weeks earlier than necessary.

She'd kept her head turned away from him for the entire trip, and neither of them had spoken.

Themba was the only home she'd ever known, but she'd never been back. Until today.

The helicopter dipped and banked sharply and suddenly there it was, beneath her feet: the rocky outcrop on the hilltop where the lions had used to laze in the sun, and the sandy riverbed, bone-dry at this time of year, before the summer rains came, and the dark smudge of the fever trees which had shaded the huts. She could see the rough imprint of the place she remembered, like in one of those aerial photographs of an ancient settlement, faint outlines beneath the surface on a modern map. The landscape was fixed, as old as time, but everything else had changed.

She'd been travelling for two days. She'd eaten a tiny amount of the plastic airline food, she hadn't slept at all, and nascent anxiety, in the form of that little flip of her stomach, had shown itself only a couple of hours out of San Diego. It had built with each leg of the journey. Now, it had a stranglehold on her which mocked all her attempts at controlled breathing, visualisation or mindful thought.

She gave in to it and gripped the leather tote on her knees.

The email from the institute which had dropped into her inbox, asking her to replace an injured colleague on this trip, had been urgent. There'd been no question of refusing the request. This was a work assignment, and she'd approach it with her usual stringent professionalism.

It was also, she told herself, an opportunity to get answers to her questions about her parents. Questions which tethered her to Themba and her past, however long her absence and however many miles she put between herself and the place where she'd grown up.

The pilot grinned at her from behind his aviator shades and pointed down, then held up three fingers, which she took to mean they'd be on the ground in three minutes. No doubt he interpreted her bloodless knuckles as a fear of flying.

He was right about her unease, but wrong—so absolutely wrong—about the root of it. Every muscle in her body was rigid with apprehension, and it annoyed the hell out of her. Because that impulsive, wild, eighteen-year-old, who'd suggested herself as a wife for Jack, no longer existed. She'd been obliterated in the past eleven years by three brilliant degrees and an astonishing ascent of her chosen career ladder. She could deliver a lecture to a hall full of restless students, address a conference of five hundred delegates or present a paper to a board of crusty professors of zoology with ice-cool confidence.

But the prospect of what lay ahead in the next few minutes had shredded her composure to bits.

Three minutes, and she didn't feel ready. But would she ever?

A rush of hot panic burned through her and she wondered if she could change her mind, return to Skukuza on the helicopter. She could be on a flight back to London this evening, possibly— tomorrow for sure.

Because three minutes meant she was about to come face to face with Jack.

Anna stared at the ground as it rose rapidly towards them. She glimpsed the striped dazzle of a herd of zebra, clouds of red dust billowing from beneath their hooves as they galloped away from the racing shadow of the helicopter. Then came the bump as the aircraft touched down on the baked earth.

The pilot pulled off his headset and turned in his seat. 'There you are. Safe and sound.'

If only he knew.

The door next to Anna slid open and a man in a

khaki bush shirt, with the name *Themba* embroidered on the pocket, gave her a half-salute.

'Welcome to Themba, Dr Kendall.'

Jack Eliot heard the far-off thump of the approaching helicopter and swore. He glanced at his watch. They were early, dammit, and he was nowhere near ready.

He'd roared back into the camp ten minutes before, after a night of hardly any sleep and a day spent in fruitless pursuit of the poachers who'd been spotted shortly before midnight. They'd melted away into the bush in the vicinity of Crooks' Corner, as they so often did. The lie of the land would have been embedded in their souls from birth, and they'd had the choice of two borders to escape over. But at least it seemed they hadn't killed anything. Not this time. If they had, he and his tracker would have spotted the telltale lazy circling of vultures, homing in on their grisly meal.

He was filthy, hot and beyond exhausted. What he wanted—*needed*—was a shower and a beer and an early night. But instead he had to entertain his guests at dinner on the deck of the Marula Restaurant in two hours' time. And before that he had to welcome a representative of the Institute for Wildlife Conservation, who had arrived on the helicopter that had already touched down, judging by the slowing beat of the rotor blades. He hoped Dan was there to meet it in the Range Rover.

It was important—make that crucial—that everything went smoothly for this visit. He'd planned it, as he did everything, down to the last detail. If you had things planned, you also had them under control. The years when his life had lurched from one crisis to another were over— had been ever since his father...

He shook his head, dragging his tired brain back to the present. Now he had to hope nothing would go wrong. Although in his experience, that particular hope was rarely fulfilled. In the bush, the opportunities for disaster were legion.

In the hands of this visitor lay the power to grant him funding to extend the research centre at Themba and to train additional staff to step up the fight against poaching. Funding, although welcome, would bring with it far more than money. It would signal international recognition of the importance of the conservation work they were doing here, and worldwide interest would follow. There'd be more jobs for local people, and opportunities for education in the rural communities. The survival of the animals, many of them endangered species, depended on it.

Jack spread his hands on the surface of his desk and pushed himself upright. He grabbed a bottle of water from the fridge and took several gulps, slaking his thirst and shifting the coating of dust in his mouth and throat. He stopped short of tipping the remaining contents of the bottle over himself. The dust in his hair would turn to mud, and besides, water was a precious resource, in short supply at the dry end of winter, when the riverbeds were cracked and parched and most of the waterholes had shrunk to puddles.

So he combed his fingers through his hair instead and washed his hands. Stubble roughened his jaw, but he couldn't do anything about that now.

Ducking his head to look out of the window, he saw the dark green Range Rover with the gold Themba crest on its side cross the low bridge and bump over the cattle grid into the camp. Then he headed out of his office and across the deck.

He paused for a moment and glanced to the west, doing his habitual weather-check. The blood-red ball of the sun hovered above a clear horizon. No clouds, so no rain yet.

The Range Rover pulled up at the foot of the steps. Dan leapt from the driver's seat and strode around to the passenger side, while another staff member stepped forward to take a leather bag from the boot.

Jack narrowed his eyes as a woman appeared around the front of the four-by-four. She wasn't what he'd expected at all, because for starters he'd been expecting a man. He kicked himself mentally for his old-fashioned, oh-so-predictable mind-set. He might have hauled Themba into the twenty-first century, but was he stuck somewhere in the Dark Ages? Doctors of zoology didn't have to be men, for God's sake. But he hadn't queried it—just assumed. They also didn't have to be grey-haired and bearded, but they didn't often come in the shape of the one who now paused at the foot of the wide, granite steps. He was certain of that because a figure like hers was one in a million.

She raised her head, and one hand moved to flatten against her chest, then it drifted across to join the other in a double-fisted grip on the strap of her shoulder bag. She placed a booted foot on the bottom step...

Anna slid out of the passenger seat before the driver had cut the ignition. Dan—her welcoming party of one—had tried to make conversation during the drive from the airstrip, and she'd tried and mostly failed to sound intelligent. Now he closed the door and followed her around the bonnet of the vehicle.

She was here, and she really, *really* needed to get this done.

At the foot of the steps she raised her eyes, tried to breathe, and tried again. Her first glimpse of

Jack's six-foot-four, wide-shouldered frame had knocked the air from her lungs.

With powerful, long thighs beneath worn cargo pants, slim hips, and a chest and shoulders broad enough to block out the light, he looked harder than she remembered—and *built*. And he looked as though he'd had a hell of a day. His dark hair, cropped short at the sides and thick with dust, was untidily raked off his forehead. Shirtsleeves rolled to the elbows revealed corded, tanned forearms, and that watch which did everything was still strapped to his wrist.

She'd thought she loved him when she was eighteen, but she was over him now—right? She'd been over him for ten years and a number of days. So why had this hot rush of grown-up, X-rated desire set her heart pumping and lit a fire in her abdomen?

Anna began the slow climb up the steps towards him…

The white cotton shirt the woman wore looked crisp and clean, and it made Jack even more uncomfortable about his own straight-out-of-the-bush appearance. A narrow red leather belt was threaded through the loops of figure-hugging slim jeans, which encased long, long, wrap-around-me legs. Her lace-up leather boots were sturdy enough for the bush, and sexy as sin teamed with such a super-sleek body.

Jack jerked his thoughts back to reality. Where had that little lapse come from? He kept his distance, mentally and especially physically, from guests, staff and business associates, and kept his libido in a grip a crocodile would envy. There was no time for any involvement that didn't concern the well-being of Themba, his staff and the animals on his land. He'd fought to make Themba into what it was today, and he was damned if he'd let his purpose stray. So he instructed his brain to stamp out the annoying flame somewhere low down in his gut reminding him that he hadn't had sex since... Since he couldn't be bothered to remember when.

The thought that she might be a guest whose arrival he'd somehow overlooked dropped into his head. He'd been absent since midnight, so he might have missed something. If that was the case, he'd have words. He liked—*demanded*—to be kept informed, about everything. No exceptions.

He scanned the road to the airstrip, but it was quiet. There was no second helicopter making an approach, no cloud of dust signalling another vehicle on its way to the lodge.

As she mounted the final step onto the deck he realised she was taller than he'd thought. He studied her for a moment, something snagging at his memory. A straight nose, a wide, full, kiss-me-now mouth fixed in serious mode, and a lightly tanned complexion. She must be exhausted after a journey of twenty-four hours, so how come she looked as if she'd just stepped out of a fashion shoot?

Dan appeared at his shoulder. 'Jack? Are you okay?' He stepped forward. 'This is…'

Single pearls gleamed in her earlobes, and something about the tilt of her chin as she looked up at him disturbed a memory buried deep. Green eyes, the colour of cold sea glass, met his. His heart lurched in his chest.

He felt Dan's hand on his arm. 'Jack?'

She extended a slim hand towards him, her eyes fixed on his face. 'Hello, Jack,' she said, her voice as cool as her eyes.

'Anna?'

The word that came out of his throat was rough and harsh. It had lodged there, never to be spoken, for so long it sounded unreal—like some made up name. He tried it on his tongue again, as he closed his fingers around her hand.

'Anna…'

She left her hand in his for a moment, then withdrew it. He inhaled and tried to find some oxygen, but there didn't seem to be any in his vicinity. His head swam, and through a haze of shock he heard Dan's voice, again.

'Jack, this is Dr Kendall, who we've been expecting. Would you like me to show her to her suite?'

Jack pulled a hand over his eyes and shook his head. 'Thank you, Dan, no. I'll…I'll take it from here.'

'Okay.' Dan sounded doubtful. 'If you're sure?' He turned away, then twisted round again. 'You were out of contact, Jack. The email only came in…'

Jack sent him a look and he shrugged and backed off, turning to take the steps down to the vehicle two at a time.

She… Anna…watched him with those frosty eyes. The last time he'd seen them they'd been sparkling like emeralds with unshed tears. She'd jerked her head backwards, so the casual farewell peck he'd steeled himself to drop on her cheek had landed somewhere in the air between them.

As he'd driven off he'd watched her in the rear-view mirror and wondered if she'd let the tears fall once he'd gone. The set of her shoulders and her ramrod spine had made him think otherwise. He'd breathed a sigh of relief, even though it had felt as if a part of him had been ripped away.

He hauled his mind back to the present—to now, and how to handle this. His brain felt sluggish, as if he was watching a slow-motion movie of himself.

He hated surprises. Most of the surprises he'd had in his life had been disasters dressed up by someone else to lessen the blow. Strangely, the only good one he could remember was Anna's first arrival at Themba, as a two-year-old orphan. With the benefit of hindsight he realised that was the day when some sort of purpose had begun to emerge from the random chaos of his childhood.

'It seems you aren't expecting me, Jack.' Her brow creased.

'I… No, I wasn't.' Just in time he stopped himself from saying he'd been expecting a man. He had the feeling such an admission wouldn't go down too well with this version of Anna. 'I…I've been in the bush for almost twenty-four hours.'

He wrapped his arms across his chest and tucked his hands into his armpits to keep them out of trouble. Because his gut reaction was to wrap them around her and hold her in an embrace which would sweep them back to the time when she'd appeared, like something miraculous, from a bundle on a woman's back. To all those years when they'd been easy together, great mates who could talk about everything and anything, before she'd grown up and an inconvenient, tantalising tension had begun to crackle between them.

Her eyes warmed by one degree of frost and she

tilted her head. The last horizontal rays from the setting sun caught her hair, slicking rose-pink over the blonde. Her hair—her glorious bright hair, which had used to ripple to her waist and fly out behind her in a banner of gold as she leapt from rock to rock, barefoot and agile as an antelope—was tamed and bound into a neat French plait. The end of the thick braid hung over her right shoulder, tied with a narrow length of black velvet ribbon.

Jack's brain finally kicked into gear. How had he missed this? There was something wrong—and it was her name. On the documentation he was sure it had said *Professor A. Scott*, and that wasn't her name. Was it? The awful thought that she might be married, to someone called Scott, made his stomach churn. Was she married? To someone called Scott? Surely he would have known by some process of telepathy if she'd got married?

That was ridiculous, of course, because he hadn't heard from her for eleven years, so how could he have known? But at least he wasn't going crazy. If her real name had been on the paperwork it would have hit him in the chest like a bolt from a stun gun.

And after he'd recovered from the shock? What would he have done?

Asked for someone else, probably, although that would've been pushing his luck with the institute, risking annoying them when he couldn't afford to.

'No,' he said again, forcing his voice into something like a normal register. 'Your name. It's not Scott.' He risked a glance at her left hand, which held the strap of her bag. No ring visible.

The small frown between her brows cleared. 'Oh, Alan Scott collided with a lamppost on his e-scooter and broke an ankle. I'm the last-minute substitute. Surely they let you know?'

'No, they didn't…' Jack stopped.

Links to the outside world were famously unreliable and they'd maintained radio silence since before midnight. That must be the email Dan had mentioned.

'I apologise for the mix-up,' Anna said, 'but right now…' She looked around, appearing to notice her surroundings for the first time. 'Right now, I've been travelling for forty-eight hours. I'm so tired I can barely stand, and I need a shower and something to eat—preferably in that order. Could you show me where I'm sleeping? I don't recognise anything any more.'

'Forty-eight hours? Was the flight from London delayed?'

She looked puzzled for a moment, then shook her head. 'No. But I started in San Diego.'

The door clicked shut and Anna finally—*finally*—released her stranglehold on her bag, dropped it on a low glass table and examined the room. Rough granite walls, painted white, disappeared up into the shadows of the steeply pitched thatched roof. The warm air moved to the slow beat of a ceiling fan.

She sank into one of the cream linen armchairs and exhaled, staring through floor-to-ceiling glass doors which opened onto a wide covered deck.

She'd held it together. Although fate, or something, had been on her side. The way Jack had been utterly blindsided by her arrival had helped her to hide her anxiety. Luckily, once she'd climbed up the steps—fourteen of them, she'd counted, and a fraction of the number she'd needed—she'd started to recover.

She'd seen the moment when frank interest had shifted to wariness in Jack's eyes, and then the shocked jolt of recognition.

She'd fought off the impulse to step forward and put her arms around him. That was how it had used to be, when she'd come home from boarding school in those long-gone, carefree days.

There was a scar she didn't remember on his forehead. She'd wanted to run her fingers over it and ask him how he'd got it. But she'd kept her cool, and she'd keep it for the next week, even if it half killed her. Her professional reputation depended on it.

Fingers clumsy with fatigue, she untied the laces of her boots, and when she finally eased them off, followed by her socks, she put her feet on the cool stone floor and felt the stress drain out of her. She could have curled up right there on the chair and slept for twelve hours. But a vast bed, made up with fine embroidered cotton, with a linen cover folded at the foot, had been turned down, inviting sleep there. Misty mosquito netting, suspended from a hoop above, hung in protective drifts around it.

Anna padded into the bathroom and changed her mind about a shower. The bath was deep and long, and she turned on the taps, tipping in a good measure of bath oil from a square glass bottle which stood on a shelf alongside other luxuries. The scent of lavender rose in the steam as she peeled off the clothes she'd been wearing for two days and a night, and slid into the silky water.

Jack closed the door to the executive suite and headed for the sanctuary of his own space. His accommodation was all that remained of the original camp, and the executive suites were close to it by design. It was where official visitors stayed, and he liked to be on hand and nearby because they were always there for business reasons.

He'd have to treat Anna in the same way he

treated all of them, but it would take a little time and a lot of effort to get used to the idea.

The old buildings among the fever trees had consisted of a group of thatched huts. He and his father had occupied one each, and when Anna had been old enough she'd had her own, too. The remainder had been used by staff, and the men who'd used to come in loud, bragging groups to shoot big game.

The kitchen had been an outside affair, with a firepit and a spit at its centre. It had been the last area Jack had updated, after building the rest of the lodge. Now he had an en-suite bathroom, a proper kitchen, and covered walkways between the huts. The old kitchen had become an outdoor seating area, around a new firepit.

Here he could relax, away from the formality of the guest lodge, and be himself. Books lined the walls, and a silver-framed photograph of his mother as a young woman stood on a side table.

He strode straight through his living room and into the kitchen, where he pulled a beer from the fridge and tugged open the ring-pull. He tipped the cold liquid down his throat, swallowed and tipped some more. If he'd thought his day difficult, it had got a whole lot more complicated in the last half an hour.

Anna. He wiped the back of a hand across his mouth and walked through the sliding doors onto his deck, gazing down at the glint of one of the last remaining patches of water in the river but not seeing it. She was back, and he felt as though he'd been trampled by a charging rhino—only he was still alive.

Eleven years ago, he'd hurt her. He knew he had. And her silence had been proof, if he'd needed it, that she'd gone for good. He'd written to her, at the only address he'd had, but he'd never heard back. In the end, he'd given up.

He'd had to make sure she left for her own safety, and he wondered if he'd find a time, in the next seven days, to explain it to her in a way that might start to heal the rift between them. Only he didn't know if she'd want that.

In that split-second moment of recognition at the top of the steps he'd been catapulted back in time, to where memories churned and raged and uncertainty ruled. He drained the can and crushed it in his fist. Then he glanced at his watch.

He had an hour to calm down, take a shower, find fresh clothes and get a grip. Then he had to spend the evening making meaningful conversation with the group of nine American ecologists who were his guests this week. They were sincere, earnest and deeply interested in the work being undertaken at Themba, in conservation, education and the frontline fight against poaching. And they'd paid handsomely for the privilege of luxury accommodation, five-star treatment and his company. They deserved his undivided attention—something he knew he was going to find difficult to give this evening.

Firstly, he'd have to stop thinking about the woman who had climbed up the steps towards him and his response to her. He'd tried to kill those feelings long ago, when she was fifteen and suddenly not a child any more. He'd put up cool defences against her and she'd made a game of trying to breach them. Only today she hadn't had to try. He should have been safe after eleven years, but those carefully built defences had crumbled at the touch of her hand, at the direct cool gaze of her eyes. They'd slipped off him, leaving him exposed and unprepared. He hated the feeling.

He stripped off his dusty, sweaty clothes, lifted some weights and ran for half an hour on the treadmill. Then he decided on a cold shower. Maybe that would bring his body to heel.

The African night had fallen with its abrupt swiftness when he stepped outside again, and it was fully dark. The nocturnal sounds of the bush were ramping up, but the dry heat still lingered. Ground-level solar lanterns glowed along the edges of the paved paths which curved through the camp. He could see golden lamplight flickering through the branches of the trees which sheltered the Marula Restaurant, where he should have been five minutes ago, ready to welcome his guests.

Quiet voices drifted towards him and he quickened his pace. Then he stopped. From the angle of the path he could see a corner of Anna's deck. Soft light spilled through the open doors of her suite, silhouetting her where she leaned her elbows on the railing. The white linen fabric of a Themba bathrobe gleamed in the dimness. Her hair, released from the constraints of that tight plait, flowed over her shoulders.

He watched her for a long minute, and then she turned her head in his direction.

'I know you're there, Jack,' she said in a low voice. 'I've always known when you were there.'

CHAPTER TWO

JACK DROPPED HIS HEAD, ran a hand over the back of his neck and swore under his breath. He pulled his phone from his pocket and tapped a message to Dan.

Keep them talking. With you in ten.

The door was unlocked, but he hesitated on the threshold. Time was when he would have walked right into Anna's bedroom without a second thought, he reflected. And she into his.

'You can come in, Jack.'

She still stood on the deck, her hands buried in the pockets of the pale bathrobe. An evening breeze rustled through the trees and lifted a corner of the fine linen, exposing a long length of butterscotch-smooth thigh to Jack's hungry gaze.

He dragged his eyes away, trying to blank the thought that the robe might be all she wore. She stepped off the deck onto the slate tiles and slid the door closed behind her.

Jack moved into the centre of the room. 'Your door should be locked.' He barely recognised his own voice. He swallowed. 'It's not safe to leave it open.'

Anna lifted her chin and smiled. Her eyes gleamed with a flash of mischief. She hadn't grown out of that—or out of the dimple in the middle of her left cheek.

'So it seems,' she said.

'No. That's not...'

What was wrong with him? She had him tied in knots and he hadn't even touched her, apart from their handshake earlier, when his world had been shaken up and then dropped around him in a shape he didn't recognise.

He dragged air into his uncooperative lungs and shook his head. 'That's not what I meant.'

She tipped her head to one side, regarding him steadily, a hint of teasing still playing at the corners of her mouth. 'Oh?'

'It's the monkeys.' He glanced away from her, out into the dark beyond the window. 'It's okay now it's dark. But during the day they'll find their way in. They've learned to open the doors.'

He watched her walk towards him. Her bare toes were tipped in a pearly shell-pink. Since when had she ever used nail polish?

She stopped and gestured towards the crisp linen chairs. 'Won't you sit down? We should probably have a conversation.'

She was too close. His body had leapt into life in a way he hadn't experienced for...well, for ever. It felt like for ever since he'd walked away from her.

He caught his bottom lip between his teeth and pushed his hands into his pockets. Feeling his phone in one of them reminded him that Dan was waiting, along with the American ecologists—waiting for him to show up for dinner and intelligent discussion.

He shook his head, relieved to have a legitimate excuse to leave. Rather than taming his wayward body and mind, the exercise and the cold shower had simply revived him. Right now, the only conversation he wanted to have with Anna would not take place on a chair...

He kept his eyes away from the gauzy mosquito netting around the bed.

'I can't stay. I'm hosting a dinner for some of the guests and I'm already late.' He shrugged. 'I'm sorry.'

'That's okay. Like I said earlier, I'm tired. And hungry.' The corners of her wide mouth lifted. 'When I've eaten and slept I'll be more like myself.'

The words that came out of Jack's mouth next weren't the ones he'd planned to say at all.

'Will that,' he asked, 'be the you I know, or this new version of yourself?'

He wished the question unasked as soon as

he'd uttered it, but it was too late. He saw a flash of something like anger in the emerald depths of her eyes.

'The version of me you see is who I am now, Jack.' She pulled her hands from her pockets and curled her fingers around the edges of the robe at her throat. 'The one you thought you knew vanished…oh, years ago.' The bones of her knuckles shone white under the taut skin. 'Did you think I'd still be a naïve eighteen-year-old? Just a *kid*?'

Something hit the slate floor, stone on stone. It skittered towards him, coming to rest near his feet. Anna made a grab for it, but Jack got there first. He straightened up and examined the small heart-shaped pebble, turning it over in his fingers. A thin diagonal band of white quartz dissected it.

'What's this?' he asked, although he already knew.

Anna straightened up and lifted her chin. She hadn't grown out of that faintly defiant gesture, either. And if he'd thought she was too close before, this was approaching lethal.

'It's…nothing. Just something that was in my pocket.' She held out a hand, palm upwards. 'Can I have it? Please?'

Jack raised his eyes and his gaze collided with hers. She didn't look away.

'It's not nothing.'

Her eyes held his. 'It's…'

'It's the pebble I gave you when you were twelve.'

She didn't deny it, but her lids dropped, hiding any emotion in her eyes.

'Isn't it, Anna?'

She gave a quick nod. 'It... I found it in my wash bag and it reminded me...*reminds* me...'

Jack looked beyond her, out into the inky darkness. 'It was down there in the riverbed, where I found you that day. Do you remember?'

Anna turned her head and followed the direction of his glance. 'Yes. I remember. I was crying...'

'You were crying because you were being sent away to boarding school.' His voice gentled. 'You were afraid.'

She turned back to look at him. 'Themba was all I knew. I couldn't imagine how I would live anywhere else, with strangers.'

Her tone was forceful, but she nipped her bottom lip between her teeth and he thought it was to stop it trembling.

Then she gave a wobbly smile. 'And I'd have to wear *shoes*.'

'You were sitting on a boulder, flinging pebbles into the water, but I rescued this one.' He smoothed a finger over the small talisman in his hand. 'Can you remember what I said when I gave it to you?'

She followed the movement of his finger. 'You said that whenever I felt lonely and homesick I should hold it in my hand and I'd know you were thinking of me and I'd be back here soon.'

Jack nodded. 'Anything else?'

Her smooth brow furrowed. 'I remember the crocodile. And how cross you were.'

'It was a monster, and it could have swallowed you whole.'

There was that impish dimple again. His stomach hollowed and his chest expanded in a deep, controlling breath.

'Only they don't swallow their prey whole, Jack. You know that.'

'Do you think drowning in the jaws of a croc is any better?'

'I'd seen him. It was a safe enough distance away. And, yes…' she held up her hand as he opened his mouth to speak again '…I do know how fast they can move. I'd worked that out, too.'

'You drove me nuts with the risks you took, Anna.'

'Ah, but you were my teacher, Jack. You and Joseph. Is he still here?'

Jack nodded. 'All our current trackers have been trained by him but he's enjoying retirement now.'

'He taught me well, too. The risks I took were always informed and calculated. I only realised later it wasn't true.'

'What wasn't true? The bushcraft we taught you was impeccable.'

'Not that.' She shrugged. 'I mean, I realised you couldn't have been thinking about me every time I was homesick, because I was homesick all the time.'

'Anna…' He wanted to tell her how wrong she was.

She stretched out her hand again. 'Can I have it back now?'

Jack's fingers closed over the pebble, then he opened his fist to let it drop into her palm. Her fingers brushed against his. He knew then that he'd been right not to touch her, because the shock jolting through him made him grip her hand, pressing the little granite heart into her skin.

She inhaled, a gasp of awareness, and Jack closed the small gap between them. She was tall, but not so tall that the top of her head didn't fit perfectly under his chin.

Her lithe body, which he'd watched grow from childhood compactness into teenaged long-leggedness, felt more rounded than he'd expected. Because it wasn't as if he hadn't imagined this. He'd dreamed of holding her long before she'd left—and long after, too. All he'd ever allowed himself had been a fleeting brush of his hand on hers, a joshing shove of a shoulder over some joke, and maybe, if he was feeling strong enough, a hug when she'd come home from school or he'd returned from university or the mine.

Her naïve attempts at flirtation had stretched his self-control to the limit. But his dreams hadn't prepared him for the reality. He'd never known it would feel like this. Their palms gripped the stone between them, but he splayed his other hand across her shoulder blades. He felt them pull down under his touch as she arched closer to him. He felt her fingers rest on his waist and all the blood in his body headed south. Her breath, quick and shallow, was warm against his collarbone.

'Anna?'

'Mmm?' She turned her head and he rested his forehead against hers.

'I haven't kissed you hello.'

'You stopped doing that when I was fifteen.'

'Yes.' He'd always wondered, stupidly, if she'd noticed.

'And I didn't kiss you goodbye.'

'No. I didn't let you.'

He moved their entwined fingers to tip her chin up with his knuckles and then ran his thumb over her bottom lip. 'So that's two kisses...'

'Jack, I...'

'Don't say anything. Please.'

He let his mouth follow where his thumb had been, feathering across her lips. This wasn't the farewell kiss he'd been going to drop on her cheek, which had never found its mark. This was meant to be a cool, contained greeting between two people who hadn't seen each other in more than a decade. But it turned into a welcome of a different kind altogether.

His hand moved up her back to tangle in the mass of her honey-streaked hair and to cup the back of her head. Then his lips, no longer gentle or tentative, fused with hers, trying to make up for all the years when he wouldn't touch her and all the years when he couldn't.

Every new curve of her body seemed to fit perfectly with his. He combed his fingers through her hair, down to her waist and beyond, clamping her hard against him. Her fingers drifted up to his chest. Their tips were cool against the heated skin of his throat. Then she slipped a hand around the back of his neck and buried her fingers in his hair, pulling him down harder and opening the seam of her lips at the invitation of his tongue.

The universe shrank to this moment, this place, and he wanted it to go on for ever.

Her skin, smooth as satin, smelled of lavender and roses and she tasted... God, she tasted sweeter than honey. He devoured her mouth, trying to satisfy a hunger which had gnawed at him for ever. The little moan in her throat inflamed him even further as she ran her fingers down his spine and spread her hand across his pelvis.

Then suddenly she was pushing against his

chest, shaking her head. She tore her mouth from under his and twisted her face away.

'Jack, no!'

Drowning in a whirlpool of sensation and raw desire, he held on to her, trying to claim her lips again, but she resisted.

'Anna, please…'

Her head shifted against his chest. 'No.'

Jack carefully let go of her and wrapped his arms around her, resting his cheek on her head. His breath was ragged as he tried to get his body under some sort of control. He could feel the race of her heart hammering against his ribs. When it had slowed down to something like normal, he slid his arms away from her and took a step back. She raised her hands, as if she was going to reach for him again, then let them drop to her sides.

Jack stared at her. She stared back, and he thought she looked appalled.

'I'm…sorry,' he muttered. 'I didn't mean that to happen. It was…' He stopped, not willing to explain just what she'd done to him.

'It wasn't just you, Jack,' she whispered. 'It was me, too. But this can't happen. It mustn't.' She shook her head. 'Not again.'

Jack pulled a hand over his face, trying to steady himself. She'd moved a little further away from him.

Safer, he thought. *But I don't want safe. Safe*

was where I was earlier, even though I'd had a terrible day. And I don't want to go back there.

He breathed in a couple of times, watching her do the same.

'Anna…' he started, then shook his head. 'I don't know how to say this.'

She moved sideways, putting one of the armchairs between them. 'I can't help you, Jack.'

'No. Only I can say sorry for the way I hurt you…before. Before you left.'

Pain flashed in her eyes before she swept her lids down. Her hand tightened around the pebble she still held in one fist, but when she looked at him again her gaze was direct and honest.

'You did. Hurt me, I mean.'

'I know. It's been hard to forget or to forgive myself. In fact, I…'

'I've found it hard to forgive you, too, Jack. You belittled me when I'd just found the courage to lay bare my deepest feelings.'

'I know, and I'm sorry, but…'

'If you remember,' she carried on, straightening her spine and shaking that shimmering mass of spun gold down her back, 'you said I was just a kid. You asked me if I was…*insane.*'

Jack remembered. Every day he remembered. Now he nodded. 'I remember. And you *were*. Just a kid. Maybe not insane, but it was an insane suggestion.'

'I was eighteen, Jack. Legally grown up. Old enough to vote. Old enough to have sex. And to get married.'

Anger stirred and started to build in Jack's gut. Fury at his dead father, because of how he'd been forced to treat her eleven years ago, and frustration at how her memory had haunted him ever since. But his overriding emotion was shock. He might have thought of her every day and many nights since their parting, but he'd always had his emotions under control. What had taken eleven years to build had taken one kiss to be destroyed. The iron grip in which he held his feelings, his heart…his *life*…had melted in the heat of one kiss. He'd lost control of all of it, and it scared him to his soul.

'You may have been eighteen, but you definitely weren't grown-up,' he snapped. 'Your range of experience was limited to Themba, where you ran wild and often wilfully in the bush, and a cloistered girls' boarding school where you had whispered giggling conversations about boys and sex in the dorm after lights out.' He took a breath. 'You needed to get away. I couldn't let you bury yourself here for ever.'

He saw by her look of shock that his words had found their mark.

'Remember,' he went on, his voice softening, 'I also went to boarding school. And your guardian wanted you to complete your education in England.'

Her slim fingers plucked at the fabric on the back of the chair and she looked up again. 'You were right, of course,' she said. 'I did have to go. But I was afraid. I barely remembered meeting George, my unofficial guardian, when I was five and he came to Themba to check up on me. I couldn't imagine what life in London would be like. I wanted to stay here, where I felt safe.'

The irony, thought Jack, was that she'd been far from safe here. He needed to explain that to her when he felt calmer and could find the words.

'And now?' he asked, making a clumsy gesture which encompassed both of them. 'Are you punishing me for that rejection when you were eighteen?'

Confusion clouded her eyes for a moment, followed by comprehension. 'No. Not at all.' She shook her head. 'I'm here to do a job, Jack. You've applied to the institute for funding and official endorsement for Themba, and this assessment I've been sent to do is part of the deal. I have to be, and be seen to be, absolutely professional and impartial in my findings. After Professor Scott was injured I was the only person available, if you want it done now—which you do.'

Hurt twisted in Jack's gut at her words. 'So you didn't *want* to come back?'

She moved around the chair and sat down, folding up her legs and tucking her feet underneath her. 'I never wanted to leave, remember?'

'That's not...' Jack's phone vibrated. The message from Dan consisted of a row of question marks and a desperate emoji face. 'I have to go.'

He took a step towards her, but she pushed out a hand.

'Stay away, Jack.'

He stopped and put a hand up to rub his eyes. 'Okay. I'll...I'll see you tomorrow, sometime. If you need anything...'

'If I need anything I'll call Reception.' She glanced at the glossy folder which lay on the coffee table. 'I'm sure all the necessary information is in there.'

He nodded. 'Of course.'

And then, with his hand on the door handle, he turned back towards her. 'Have you eaten? Ordered food?'

'Not yet. But I will—if the lure of that bed doesn't get to me first.'

Jack swallowed. Did she *have* to mention the bed? He nodded again and pulled the door open. With a last glance at her he stepped into the night.

She'd pulled her hair over one shoulder and was weaving it into a thick plait. It gleamed like shot silk in the lamplight.

'Try to stay awake until you've had a meal. And don't forget to lock the door,' he said, as he closed it behind him.

Jack strode along the shadowy path towards the Marula Restaurant. Raucous laughter drifted through the dark and he felt a stab of guilt at having left Dan to entertain the buttoned-up ecologists. But by the sound of it some of them had relaxed in Dan's care.

He tried to order his mind, to put the importance of discussing the work they were doing at Themba before the soaring and unreasonable demands of his body. Control was something he needed in all areas of his life and at all times. He'd thought he'd mastered the art. But eleven years had dulled the memory of how Anna could test it, with her flirtatious glances and teasing games. She'd had no idea of his fierce desire for her and how he'd fought to control it. And now one touch had brought it flashing back, sharper than a hunter's knife.

He mounted the steps up to the restaurant's deck and found Dan waiting at the top.

'What's happened, mate? You look beat.' Dan frowned, his welcoming expression fading. 'Are you okay?'

Jack pinned on his best, most professional

smile and hoped he'd be able to keep it in place. 'Sorry, Dan. Something came up.'

If only he knew.

It was going to be a long night. And as for the week—that hadn't even started.

In spite of her fatigue, Anna's anger simmered. Did Jack think he could pick up with her where they'd left off before she'd made that disastrous proposal? That she was still a naïve, inexperienced teenager who would hang on his every word and do as he said?

That kiss…

She drew in a sharp breath at the memory of it. She knew she was as responsible for it as he was. She'd wanted it as much as he had. Her fingers traced across her lips as she remembered the intoxicating taste of his mouth and how his scent, unchanged over the years, had swamped her with memories.

But she'd come to her senses before he had. If she hadn't pushed him away, that kiss would have gone stratospheric. Just a few more seconds and she wouldn't have been able to stop herself.

She made a determined effort to calm down, rolling her shoulders to release the tension in her neck. But before she could reach for the folder and order a meal, there was a tap on the door.

When she opened it a staff member carried a tray into the suite and placed it on the low table.

'With Mr Eliot's compliments.'

Jack had remembered exactly what she liked. Before Anna removed the silver dome from the dish she could smell the buttery omelette which lay beneath it, golden and fluffy. A salad of crunchy green leaves and tender tomatoes, perfectly dressed, filled an earthenware bowl. A frosted bottle of Cape Sauvignon Blanc nestled in a bucket of ice.

Anna sipped from the glass the waiter had poured for her before gliding silently from the suite and sighed. She touched her fingers to her lips again. They were sensitive, and a little swollen, and she tipped her head back against the cushions of the chair and took another mouthful of the ice-cold wine.

Her response to Jack's kiss had shocked and shaken her. Had she honestly believed she'd forgotten how he could make her feel simply by brushing his hand against hers? He'd said she was just a kid when she was eighteen, but hadn't she grown up at all? When he'd rejected her and packed her off with undignified haste to cold, dark, wintry London, she'd gathered up her shredded pride and vowed that nobody would ever make her feel belittled, silly, *crushed*, again.

To date, nobody had.

Her desperate antidote to the unbearable longing she'd felt for the African bush, for Themba,
for Jack, had been to plunge headlong into academic life, burying herself in work and research,
and she'd come out with a set of astounding qual-
ifications and the world of zoology as her oyster.
Offers of research posts, lectureships and fellow-
ships had filled her inbox and she'd chosen the
best of them.

'What *drives* you?' a curious academic had
once probed, when she'd submitted her disser-
tation ahead of the deadline and in immaculate
order.

She'd smiled and shrugged. The truth—which
she'd never reveal to anyone—was that she'd
wanted to prove herself, over and over again, so
that one day she could return to Themba and
prove to Jack that she was no longer a kid, and
definitely not insane.

And then she'd leave again. Because what she'd
decided she wanted most in the world was something very different from life at Themba with
Jack.

She hadn't intended to return this way, but the
visit would serve its purpose.

She just hadn't considered that it would be so
gut-churningly, heart-wrenchingly difficult.

Until the first leg of her journey, when her return to Themba had become an unavoidable re-

ality, she hadn't doubted she could handle Jack. After all, what she'd felt for him had been nothing more than a teenage crush. But somewhere in the skies over Wyoming she'd begun to wonder if she'd got that completely wrong.

By the time she'd reached the top of that flight of fourteen steps to the deck she'd known for sure she had. Because that crush had grown up along with her, and now it was hot, adult desire which flared into life the moment their hands touched. This wasn't the puffy clouds and pink hearts her teenaged self had imagined. This was hot and dangerous and unstoppable.

Every cell of her body wanted him. How could she have known they'd fit together so seamlessly? For those few brief moments in his arms she'd felt as if she'd found what she'd been searching for before she'd even known she was looking. As if she'd come home.

The omelette melted in her mouth—the perfect food for someone who was too tired to eat. After two glasses of the crisp, light wine lethargy seeped into her veins, relaxing her tired limbs and overactive brain, and the pot of smoky bush tea was the perfect calming end to the meal.

Jack's memory could not be faulted.

Anna slipped between the cool sheets and listened to the night sounds of the bush. A hippo grunted in the riverbed and another answered from further downstream. She shivered and pulled the linen sheet up around her shoulders as the high-pitched cackle of a hyena, celebrating a successful hunt curdled the air. Every sound carried a memory. Some were clear, some long buried, but they were all of Jack and those nights when they'd lain in a hammock, head to toe, outside the huts, identifying the noises and calls of the animals.

Then one holiday the hammock had gone. Jack had said it had got worn out and been thrown away, but he'd sounded unconvincing and she'd never quite believed him.

She relived their kiss for the hundredth time and shifted restlessly, turning over to reach for a sip of water. The memory of his jaw, freshly shaved, hard against her face, made her put her fingers to her cheek. To her shock, he'd smelled just as she remembered. That mix of woody citrus and intangible male had sent her head spinning and her hand pushing into his hair, dragging him closer, crushing his mouth harder against hers.

Kissing him hadn't been part of the plan. She was supposed to be going to be cool, grown-up and professional. But she'd been swamped by the power of chemistry. She hadn't expected Jack's memory to be so...*whole*.

From the day he'd given her that pebble it had stayed with her. It had been in her glittery pink pencil case at school. At university she'd kept it in a pocket in her backpack, with lip balm and make-up. When she travelled it was always in her washbag or her jewellery roll.

Jack remembered it too, and the knowledge had floored her.

Jack hadn't forgotten what she liked.

The hardest part of the coming week was going to be keeping herself out of range of his gravitational force. Her professional reputation depended on it.

CHAPTER THREE

SHORTLY AFTER DAWN the tumbling liquid call of a coucal drew Anna onto the deck, the wood cool under her bare feet.

Chattering monkeys clustered in the leafy canopy above. One, bolder than the rest, landed on the railing and eyed her, scratching an armpit. She shooed it away. It leapt onto a nearby branch and swung through the trees, protesting loudly.

Back inside, she made a cup of coffee in the state-of-the-art Italian machine, checked her inbox and found a welcoming email from the Themba research centre, with a schedule of the investigative work to be undertaken, which would form the framework of her report.

There was no sign of Jack.

Sandwiches, coffee and mineral water were delivered to her at the research centre at lunch time, and the staff there were on hand to provide her with any material she needed. She was being left to get on with her work, which suited her just fine. What had happened between her and Jack the previous night had been an aberration. Circumstances had combined with emotions, the mix resulting in an eruption of feeling that had momentarily robbed her of reason and good sense.

After a night's sleep, and with food in her tummy, she felt strong and clear-headed—which was excellent, because what she needed was to get this job done and get out of here as quickly as possible.

Hours later, Anna flipped her laptop closed. She pushed it aside and propped her elbows on the table, cupping her chin in the palm of one hand. From where she sat, in the deep shade of the research centre veranda, the view of khaki-coloured bush and wide-open sky shimmering in the afternoon heat seemed to stretch for ever.

This was not, she reflected, the best spot for concentrated work or the serious study of spreadsheets, goals and projections. Beyond the perimeter fence was a waterhole, and waterholes were the bush equivalent of the office water cooler. At some point during the day everyone turned up for refreshment and a bit of socialising. Giraffes, their legs splayed at impossible angles, stretched their necks low to drink. In the distance the outriders for a herd of elephants made their stately way towards the pool, smoky dust wreathing their feet. And skittish antelope, far more than she could count, milled about in the dun-coloured scrub, taking turns at the water.

It was easier to watch the slow drift of game than to focus on the work she should be doing. Especially when images from the past kept butting in on her train of thought. If she raised her eyes and looked to the left she could see the rocky outcrop that she and Jack had used to climb. They'd find a hidden cleft in the sun-warmed boulders and settle down to read, spot game and talk—until the day the lions had claimed it as their own personal sun lounge.

Jack had carried her up there the first time, when she was only three, giving her a piggyback ride, with her arms clasped around his neck and his elbows hooked under her bare legs and feet. It was one of her earliest memories. As a child she hadn't been able to define her emotions, but now she knew she'd felt safe and wanted. And, yes, cherished.

To Anna, the word 'home' had meant Themba. There'd never been anywhere else she'd felt she belonged. But with a few words eleven years ago Jack had dashed her teenage dreams of staying there for ever.

It had been inevitable that someone like her, orphaned and rootless, should crave the things she'd never had—a home and family of her own that would complete her, maybe fill the hollow ache of loss she'd lived with for as long as she could remember. But Jack had made it clear she wasn't going to find what she wanted, what she needed, at Themba.

'I don't want a wife. Not ever.'

His words had cut through her heart and incinerated her youthful dreams.

She reached for the pair of binoculars she'd brought with her and raised them to her eyes.

That clean, fresh scent tickled her nostrils and the skin on the back of her neck shivered. Was it her imagination playing tricks, or had her thoughts conjured him up out of the warm air?

'What can you see?'

Her heart kicked as Jack's voice behind her made her fingers tighten. The binoculars shifted out of focus and she put them down.

Would he dare to touch her shoulder, even for a second? If he did she'd slap his hand away.

When nothing happened she released a steady breath and turned her head a fraction. In her peripheral vision she saw Jack pull out a chair and sit down at the table.

Good. Perhaps he'd taken her words on board last night.

She lifted the glass of water at her elbow and took a mouthful, slaking the dryness in her throat and delaying the moment she'd have to answer his question.

Jack took the binoculars and adjusted their focus with those long, capable fingers. She shifted on the chair as she remembered the pressure of them across her shoulder blades. And the way her body had reacted.

'I gave you these for your eighteenth birthday.'

It was a statement rather than a question and she didn't need to answer.

'There's a magnificent kudu bull coming down to the water.' He stretched an arm out to the right. 'Over there. And a couple of nyala.'

'I thought,' said Anna at last, 'I saw a sable antelope.'

Jack shook his head. 'No, it's a roan...'

Anna reached for the binoculars. 'I don't think so. If you look...'

He eased the binoculars from her grasp, but instead of raising them to his eyes he put them on the table. 'It's a long time since we played the *What animal is that?* game.'

'I'm here to work, not to play childhood games.' She kept her eyes on the view of the waterhole and her tone cool.

She wished she'd put on something more sophisticated than skinny jeans and a big linen shirt. Her hair hung over her left shoulder in a thick braid. Why hadn't she taken more care and tamed it into a grown-up knot? Because showing Jack how she'd grown up was on her list of things to achieve while she was here—along with proving to him that she wasn't insane.

He glanced at the closed laptop. 'I wouldn't want to interrupt.'

'I came here with the best intentions, but the view is distracting.'

'I came to apologise.'

Anna turned her head a little to glimpse his profile. His expression was sombre, his mouth a straight line.

'Oh?'

'Yes. Last night…'

'Was a mistake. It won't happen again.' She leaned forward, pressing her folded arms onto the table. 'It was unprofessional of me.'

'It wasn't one-sided. Seeing you again was a shock, and I was already stressed. Bit of a combustible mix, as it turned out.'

Anna shrugged, trying not to think about the touch of his fingers on her heated skin, the taste of him on her lips. She wanted it all again, and more.

'Any hint of…of emotional attachment between us would jeopardise the authenticity of my report and compromise my professional standing. I have to be completely impartial.'

'I understand.'

'Coming back was perhaps more emotional than I expected it to be.' On a scale of one to ten for accuracy, that statement scored about fifteen. 'And I was tired and on edge.'

Whoever said you learned from your mistakes was massively wrong. Kissing Jack had been one of the biggest mistakes she'd ever made, but she'd make it all over again, given the chance. And again.

Jack nodded. 'I could see you were shattered. I feel I took advantage...'

'Let's just agree we were both at fault and we won't let it happen again.' She turned her eyes back to the view. The elephants were closer, several babies trotting fast to keep up with the herd. 'Thank you for the meal. Good memory, Jack.'

'Mostly.' He stood up, pushing the chair back. 'I'll leave you to work.'

Anna tapped the slim laptop with her knuckles. 'There's a lot to get through.'

'Let me know if you need anything.'

He stretched out a hand towards her and then let it fall to his side.

'Thanks. I will.'

Except what I need right now is you...

'What I need is not to be distracted by the view.' She flipped the laptop open and stared at the screen.

Jack moved behind her, heading to the door. 'Anna?'

She swivelled her head and their eyes met across the space.

'My visitors leave tomorrow, and this evening we're taking them for farewell sundowners in the bush. Will you join us?'

Anna nipped her bottom lip between her teeth. 'Do you think that's a good idea?'

'If you want to come, yes. You'll be chaperoned by nine earnest American ecologists.'

A sunset trip into the bush was something she'd never been able to resist. Judging by Jack's powers of recall he wouldn't have forgotten that, either. She didn't want to be alone with him. Her responses to him were too unstable, too volatile. His presence switched her senses onto high alert, sending her mind to places that had been off-limits for eleven years. But if she refused to go he'd think she was afraid to be with him.

'Okay, Jackson. What time do we leave?'

Jack shut himself in his office and walked to the window. But instead of the dusty road and dried-up watercourse it was Anna he saw in his mind's eye, sitting on the veranda, her feet drawn up, her arms wrapped around her shins.

He pressed the heels of his hands into his eyes to rub away the image but it didn't help. Being close to her disturbed and electrified him all at once. The ache he'd thought he'd banished was back, bigger and more troublesome than ever.

When he'd expelled Anna from his life he'd been unprepared for the impact of the gap she'd left behind. His mother's death when he was eight had buried him in grief and guilt so intense it had bewildered him. Two years later Anna's un-expected arrival had blunted it and given him a focus as he'd vowed to keep her safe at all costs.

But with her gone too the pain of loss had sharpened again, like a blade twisting in his heart.

Feeling in danger of being overwhelmed by it, he'd turned to the one thing he knew he could control. Work. He'd poured all his energy and determination into his efforts to turn Themba into a place he could be proud of, despite his father's bitter opposition. But still he'd seen the shimmer of Anna's hair in the flash of sun on water, heard her laugh on the wind and her soft footstep on the deck. It had taken weeks, months—*years*— for him to stop wondering what she was doing at any given minute of the day. But in the end he'd done it. Or he thought he had.

He'd had all night and all morning to decompress after the shock of Anna's reappearance. He'd hardly slept, in spite of his fatigue, and he'd had a hard time holding on to his temper at breakfast in the face of a trivial query from a visitor. Was the honey organic and if so could he verify that fact? Yes, and yes, but he had more pressing matters to deal with. He'd handed the query over to Dan and excused himself.

After what had happened between them last night he'd mentally armed himself against the magnetism of her allure. He'd planned their encounter at the research centre to ensure he could control their next meeting. He had to let her know, somehow, that their kiss would not be repeated. It had been difficult, but they'd drawn boundaries and he was hell-bent on sticking to them.

The fact that he hadn't dragged her into his arms, spun her round and claimed her mouth for his own he considered a good start.

He'd held back on his invitation to join the sundowners party until he'd felt confident he had himself and his reaction to Anna tied down. And then she'd swept the ground from beneath his feet and the breath from his body with the use of her old nickname for him. Nobody else in the world had the right to call him Jackson, and hearing it on Anna's lips again had rocked his universe and thrown the strength of his resolve into deep doubt.

He glanced towards the calendar on the wall. Six days to go.

The long-wheelbase vehicle with banked seating and a canvas canopy bumped off the track and across the rough scrub. Jack forced himself not to watch it.

He checked the table which had been set up under an umbrella thorn. Several staff members in Themba polo shirts stood behind it, ready to mix sundowners. The vehicle they'd arrived in, with the folding table and cold boxes of drinks and food, was tucked out of sight, behind a shrubby clump of mopane.

The site was on a promontory at a bend in the

river, and three trackers stood guard at strategic points in the bush, rifles across their backs, just in case the gathering piqued the interest of any inquisitive animals. As always, their instructions were to alert him first, so the guests could be moved to safety in the vehicles.

Once, they'd had to sit it out while a herd of elephants ambled across their chosen patch. The guns were there to reassure the guests. Firing one of them would always be an absolute last resort.

He looked down the steep bank to the river. Two crocs sunbathed on the rocks, one with its mouth wide open. Jack narrowed his eyes and could just make out a tiny plover, giving the big reptile's teeth a clean. In a muddy pool the ears, eyes and nostrils of a wallowing hippo broke the mirror surface of the water. There were probably more of them, submerged, but at the moment everything was calm.

He scanned the surrounding bush, always alert. His eyes, honed by years of practice, would pick up on anything out of place.

The engine of the game-viewing vehicle died and Jack allowed himself to look across at it. Because everything was calm except for him. What if Anna had decided not to come after all? And why did he care if she'd bailed out? He wanted her to see the best of Themba in action, that was why. He needed her to write a five-star report, recommending that Themba receive all the support and endorsements he'd requested, of course.

Then he told himself to shut up and get real. He cared because he wanted her near him all the time. He felt as if he'd denied himself his favourite drink for eleven years. Now it was within reach, and his thirst for it was all-consuming. He wanted to study her clear profile and marvel at how it was the same but subtly different. Her mouth looked softer, fuller, because her jawline was more determined. High cheekbones gave her face sculpted definition. He wanted to ease her hair out of that braid, or French plait, whatever tight restriction she'd imposed on it, and thread his fingers through it again from root to tip. Mostly he wanted to gaze into the cool green pools of her eyes without feeling he should look away after five seconds. He'd always been fascinated by how they were a paler, delicate mint at the edges, transforming to unfathomable emerald depths at the centre. Depths in which he'd willingly drown.

He was in so much trouble.

'...seven, eight, nine.'

That was all the ecologists accounted for. His stomach dropped with disappointment and he walked towards the vehicle to ask Dan what had happened. Had she simply not turned up at the meeting point? Had she offered any explanation?

'Dan? Did you...?'

'Hi, Jack.'

He swung round. His eyes landed on her boots, then travelled up, and up, and…

'Anna.' He held out a hand but she jumped down from the bottom step on her own, landing next to him.

He wished he knew what that perfume was she wore. If he could find out he'd buy her a gallon. Or, better still, buy up the brand so no one but Anna could use it, ever. She had on the same slim jeans she'd worn earlier, but she'd swapped the big linen shirt for a kaftan-style top. It fell to mid-thigh and the colour of the silk exactly matched her eyes. Was it the lighter part of her eyes or the darker? He couldn't be sure. All he *could* be sure of was that he wouldn't allow himself to get close enough to find out.

'This is amazing.' She looked around, her gaze taking in the drinks table and the staff already beginning to dispense cocktails and snacks. 'A great position and well-protected, I see. A bit different from the sundowner trips we used to take in the old Defender.'

There hadn't been any guards back then. Everyone had been responsible for their own security and there'd never been an accident. Until his father…

He shut down that avenue of thought before corrosive guilt could start to gnaw at him.

He raised an eyebrow and shrugged. 'We can't have any ecologists eaten for dinner. Although it would be the ultimate example of recycling, it would also be very bad publicity.'

'Yes, I can see the headlines now.' There was that dimple. 'The Circle of Life would take on a whole new meaning.'

'The guards are all trained trackers. They can spot an out-of-place shadow or a leaf moving when there's no breeze. We're confident we could get everyone into the vehicles before a proper problem developed.'

'Really?'

'Yeah. Come and get a drink.'

Jack forced himself to mingle among the guests, but his eyes kept straying, searching for Anna. He watched her move easily from one group to another, nodding at something that was said, contributing her own opinions. She held a glass in her fingers and took an occasional sip. She was practised at this, perfectly comfortable and confident.

The shy, leggy teenager who'd made a habit of hiding from strangers had vanished. It had been her very elusiveness that had made her so tantalising to the men who'd paid to hunt with his father. Her invisibility had put her in the greatest danger.

Realising he'd lost sight of her, Jack threaded his way through the group, needing to know where she was. His hackles rose. She'd been separated from the party by a man who was now standing too close to her for comfort. Well, for

Jack's comfort anyway. He changed direction and headed towards them.

'And what brings you here...' the man, Professor Watkins, waved his glass '...to this not exactly uncivilised place? The champagne is excellent. Perhaps "isolated" would better describe it.'

Jack watched as a little frown drew Anna's brows together.

She took a small step back. 'I'm on a research trip.'

To Jack's ears her tone was neutral, but her body language said *Keep your distance*.

'Ah! An undergraduate? And what is your specialism?'

The man had his eyes fixed on her face—*who could blame him?*—and a stab of possessiveness so sharp it caught at his breath twisted in Jack's soul.

'Oh, big cats. Although all the fauna and flora at Themba deserve special attention.'

The professor proffered his hand. 'I'm Professor Watkins. Miss...?'

Driven by the need to insert himself between Anna and the other man, Jack stepped forward. 'Allow me, Professor Watkins, to introduce Anna Kendall—*Dr* Anna Kendall. She's researching the Themba model and reviewing our methods. Anna, meet Professor Watkins.'

A faint flush spread across the man's cheeks.

Anna shook his hand but he drew back, his eyes flicking to Jack's face.

'Very pleased to meet you. I'll have to look you up.' He drained his glass and turned away, joining another group.

Jack watched him go before returning his attention to Anna. 'Sorry about that. He was—' The expression on her face stopped him short. Her eyes snapped with irritation.

'What did you think you were doing?'

He saw her jaw lift a fraction.

'He was harassing you. I was trying...

'*Harassing* me?' she cut in. 'Hardly, Jack. He was showing a polite interest.' Anna pushed a hand into the pocket of her jeans as tension squared her shoulders. 'And even if he *had* been harassing me, that wouldn't have been a cue for you to barge in like a hippo protecting its calf.'

'The hell it would. He was too close to you and I could see you weren't comfortable. I—'

'His sense of personal space was different from mine. That's all it was. And I'm more than capable of taking care of myself. I didn't need you to interfere, whatever your reasons.' She took a sip from her glass and eyed him over the rim. 'You embarrassed him, and if he's looking for something to complain about when he returns to the States he's going to start with you.'

Jack knew she was right. His response had been unreasonable and, worse, uncontrolled. His inner voice reasoned that he'd leapt to Anna's defence because that was what he'd always done, but he knew there was more to it than that. He'd been unable to deal with the sight of her showing even mild interest in another man—a man who probably lived in a proper house, who worked normal hours and ticked many of the boxes Anna might have lined up for herself.

Her irritation was justified, and he was wrong to have embarrassed a guest. Very wrong. He didn't recall ever having done it before. The customer was always right. Always.

Anna's eyes remained fixed on him and he knew he had to respond, but he was damned if he was going to apologise.

'I thought I was getting you out of a tricky situation,' he said, distracted by the shades of green in her steady gaze. Did her eyes go darker when she was angry? Or would another kind of passion…? He stopped that thought in its tracks. It was just the effect of the light, fading from afternoon to evening.

'I don't need rescuing, Jack. Not any more.' She dropped her eyes and swirled the wine in her glass. 'When I wanted you to look after me you sent me away to London—where I knew nobody and almost died of shock when the first blast of winter hit me outside Heathrow.'

Then she smiled, making his heart turn over.

'That,' she continued, 'was when I began to learn how to look after myself.'

'I'm sorry.' How the hell had that happened? He had sworn he wasn't going to apologise. 'I won't interfere again.' He half turned away from her. 'I need to be sociable.'

Jack walked away, seething. Anna's words stung, but he couldn't argue with her. Accepting that she no longer needed his protection would take a while to process. He felt a surge of annoyance at the group of guests, and suddenly couldn't wait for them to leave. Then perhaps he'd be able to concentrate and get things into some sort of perspective.

Until then he wasn't letting any of them near her again, however capable she thought she was.

Elongated shadows stretched over the winter-brown grass as the sun sank towards the western hills. The visitors drifted in twos and threes over to the truck for their return journey to the lodge and their farewell dinner. Jack counted them up the steps and Dan stood in the driver's footwell and double-checked with a headcount of his own.

'Nine.' He squinted down. 'We're missing one, Jack. It's Dr Kendall.'

Jack scanned the clearing. He couldn't see her and apprehension squeezed his chest, adrenaline already pumping. Had she wandered off, like she used to, sending his anxiety levels rocketing skywards and suppressed panic drying his mouth and making his hands shake?

He breathed in slowly and looked again, more carefully, and breathed out as he spotted her in animated conversation with one of the staff members behind the drinks table. The employee saw him looking and tipped her head in his direction, smiling. He heard Anna laugh, and then she turned and walked out of the shadow of the thorn tree towards him.

The staff would pack up the table and cold boxes after the guests had left, and he'd join them in the service vehicle for the short trip back. The trackers had moved in from their posts and one of them climbed onto the game-spotting seat mounted at the front of the truck, his rifle across his knees. The remaining two stood watching over the staff.

Everyone knew the role they had to play and it worked. He'd made sure of that.

'Sorry, Jack.' Anna reached the steps. 'Alice was telling me about the small business her mother has set up.'

She glanced up into the open-sided truck and Jack followed her gaze. The remaining empty seat was next to Professor Watkins.

It took a heartbeat for Jack to decide that this was unacceptable. He could suggest she ride back with him, in the service vehicle, but that would be too damn obvious. He thought fast.

'Dan?'

'Yup?'

'I'm going to walk back. There's still half an hour of light left and that's more than I need.'

'Sure.' Dan reached behind his seat and pulled another rifle from the metal box bolted to the floor. 'Here you go. Call me on the radio if you have a problem.'

Jack slung the weapon over one shoulder, keeping his hand on the canvas strap. He was aware of Anna's eyes on him as he adjusted it, and then he let himself look at her. Her face was alight with enthusiasm.

'I'd like to come with you,' she said.

Jack tried to keep his expression neutral. He was sure if he'd demanded she accompany him she'd have refused. He hesitated, then allowed faint indecision to colour his voice.

''I'm not sure…' He glanced down at her feet.

'My boots are sturdy enough, but if you don't want me to come…' She turned back towards the vehicle, placing one foot on the bottom step.

'You're welcome to walk with me if you think you're up to it.'

Anna moved her foot back to the ground. 'Is that a challenge?'

'Not at all. But you haven't been in the bush for over a decade. It's natural you'd be cautious. Or even afraid.'

'I've never been afraid.' Her steady gaze held

his. 'I've missed all this.' The sweep of her arm encompassed the wide landscape and the sky. 'There may not be another chance for a walk at sunset.'

'Possibly not…' Jack raised his voice and called to Dan. 'Dr Kendall has opted to come with me.' He pushed his free hand into a pocket of his combat trousers. 'We'll take the old track, along the line of the river.'

Dan gave them a thumbs-up and gunned the motor of the big vehicle into life. It roared and then settled into a steady throb as he eased it into gear. Jack watched it pull away before strolling across to where the packing up was almost complete, to let the staff know the change of plan. Then he tilted his head towards the river.

'Let's go. Do you remember the rules?'

'Stay close, do exactly as you say and never, ever run—because anything in the bush you need to run from can run faster,' Anna recited.

Jack nodded. 'It looks as though there might be a spectacular sunset. Maybe those clouds will bring us some rain.'

The track wound through the bush, at times almost disappearing under dry grass and powder-soft dust. Thorny branches crowded in close on both sides, but the chain of pewter puddles in the riverbed could be glimpsed through them. The evening bush orchestra was tuning up, the bass grunts from the hippos a steady counterpoint to the treble calls of birds.

Jack set an easy pace, scanning the surroundings, alert for anything that might spell danger. He glanced sideways at Anna's profile. Her chin was lifted, her mouth set.

She pulled a hand from her jeans pocket and tucked a wisp of hair behind her ear. 'Walking back wasn't your original plan, Jack. Were you going to ask me to come with you?'

Jack knew he wouldn't get away with fudging this. She knew exactly what he was doing, and it was precisely what they'd already argued about.

'Yes, I was. I didn't want you sitting next to the professor.' He went on the attack. 'But you know that.'

'I think you're overreacting. And, like I said…'

'Yeah, I know—you can look after yourself. And maybe I did overreact. But I walk whenever I can. You know that, too.' He stopped and shifted the rifle on his shoulder. 'Keeping my senses honed takes constant practice and it keeps everyone safer.'

'I wouldn't have come if I hadn't wanted to. And I would have happily sat next to Professor Watkins.'

Jack smiled. 'I think I'm beginning to understand that.'

He started walking again, more quickly, and Anna skipped to keep up with his long stride.

'Slow down a bit, please.'

'Sorry.'

Jack kept his eyes on the track ahead. The senses he needed to use to keep them safe were being swamped by the way the low rays of the sun gave her hair a lick of pink and how her elusive scent reminded him of green shade and blowsy roses, a million miles from the dusty bush.

'Better?'

He glanced down at her. Was it only twenty-four hours since those lips had surrendered to his questing mouth? It felt like a lifetime. It'd be so easy to stop right here and do it again. Not another soul would see them. But they'd agreed that shouldn't happen.

He dragged his attention back to reality, berating himself for letting it wander. And when his eyes returned to the track he saw why he shouldn't have allowed himself to be distracted. A moment's inattention to their surroundings had led them both, quite literally, into the jaws of danger.

His fingers on the rifle strap clenched into a fist. His free hand grabbed Anna's upper arm and dragged her to a stop beside him.

'Jack! That hurts! What're you doing?' She tried to pull away but he tightened his grip, pulling her into his side and then sliding his arm around her shoulders to keep her there.

'Oh!'

Her shocked exclamation was too loud.

'Shh!' he hissed. 'And remember the rules.'

The big male lion which had padded out of the shadows stopped in the middle of the track. His huge head, framed in a thick, dark mane, swung in their direction and his yellow unblinking eyes fixed on them. His tufted tail flicked from side to side.

Jack tightened his arm around Anna and swore under his breath. She pressed her cheek into his shoulder and he felt a tremor of tension shake her. Her breathing became shallow as her heartbeat picked up, hammering against his ribs. She was afraid, and she needed to be, and it was his fault entirely. His attention had lapsed and now he didn't know how this would play out…or if it was going to end well for themselves or for the magnificent beast that now blocked their path, sizing them up.

The two-way radio was in his back pocket, but he couldn't let go of the gun and didn't want to let go of Anna to reach it. After such a long time away he couldn't be sure she wouldn't run, and that could tip this disastrous situation over into a catastrophe.

'Jack?' she whispered.

The tone of her voice took him spinning back down the years to when they were growing up together. She'd never doubted he'd look after her then—get them out of trouble, make things right. Her trust in him had been absolute, and sometimes ill-founded, but he'd never failed her. Until this moment.

In his mind he was back at the door of the hut, watching the women unwrap the bundle inside the patterned blanket they'd carried into the compound. Grubby little fists and feet had emerged, and then a head of blonde corkscrew curls. Intrigued, he'd crept closer. A pair of green eyes above a pert nose and a rosebud mouth had fixed on his face and the toddler had held out her arms to him.

'Up,' she'd said. 'Up!'

He'd picked her up and she'd buried her face in his neck and gripped his tee shirt with strong fingers. She'd felt like a miracle—a golden child emerging from a bundle carried on a woman's back—and he'd known he'd protect her for ever. With his life if necessary. He hadn't been able to save his mother, but he would save her.

His gaze fixed on the tawny predator twenty meters away, Jack automatically calculated how quickly the big cat could close the distance between them. Too quickly, was the answer. He felt Anna's cheek hard against his collarbone again, and knew he'd protect her whatever the danger. Taking care of her was hard-wired into him, body and soul.

Inch by inch, he eased the rifle from his shoulder, knowing that if he moved too quickly he might startle the lion into aggression, and too slowly might see it coming closer, to inspect them more carefully. Neither of those things would be a good result.

Anna's head shifted a fraction and he tightened his hold on her.

'Jack, he's so beautiful...' she breathed.

What the hell? Staring a gruesome death in the face, and she thought it was beautiful?

'Keep still,' he murmured. 'And keep very quiet.'

A few more inches and the barrel of the rifle would be in his hand.

'Don't shoot, Jack. Please. We're in his space.'

With painstaking slowness he lifted the rifle to his shoulder, squinting down the sights. He saw the lion's muscles ripple under the sleek skin, the haunches tense, ready to spring.

His finger curled, tightening around the trigger.

CHAPTER FOUR

THE CRACK OF a rifle-shot split the air, reverberating off the nearby rocky cliffs. Jack heard someone shout. A cloud of weaver birds chattered out of the trees, leaving their nests swaying over the riverbed.

Over five hundred pounds of big cat twisted in mid-spring. The animal landed on his feet with a roar and bounded into the bush. In seconds he was swallowed by the dense undergrowth.

Jack lowered the barrel of the gun and relaxed his trigger finger, keeping his narrowed eyes fixed on the spot where he'd seen the tip of the lion's tail vanish. Anna's rigid shoulders sagged a fraction inside the iron band of his arm. She inched her cheek away from his collarbone and followed the direction of his gaze.

'You missed him,' she breathed.

Was that relief he could detect beneath the shakiness of her voice?

He shook his head. 'I didn't miss. I didn't fire. I don't know who did. Whoever it was…'

A khaki-clad figure materialised out of the deep shadow of a thorny thicket. He balanced a rifle on his shoulder as he walked down the track towards them.

'It's Alex.' Jack flipped on the safety catch of his gun and slung it across his back. 'One of the trackers on the staff vehicle.'

He let the arm which still bound Anna against him slide down. She moved away from his side and he fought the urge to pull her back in. Partly to protect her, but also because the way her body fitted with his felt natural, and right, and he needed the contact.

'Jack? You okay?' Alex's voice was calm and steady, at odds with his super-alert attitude. His eyes scanned the bush, his head cocked for sounds of danger. He stopped a few paces in front of them and looked at Anna. 'And you, Dr Kendall?'

Anna nodded. 'I...I'm fine, thank you, Alex. A bit shaken but...fine.'

Jack squinted at him into the sunset. 'Where did you come from? You were supposed to be on the staff transport.'

Alex shrugged. 'That lion crossed the road in front of us. I reckoned he'd intercept this old track just about the time you were level with his path.' He gestured behind him. 'I hopped off the vehicle to track him and it seems I was right.' He pulled off his wide-brimmed hat, swiped his arm across his brow and slapped the hat back onto his head. 'Michael stayed with the vehicle so they were covered. They should be back in the camp by now.'

Jack nodded. 'Did you aim...?'

'I aimed high and I shouted to distract him. I could see you had him in your sights. I figured if my shout and high shot didn't put him off you'd still have time for a last resort shot.' He grinned. 'Just.'

'Maybe.' Jack gripped his rifle strap. 'It was close. Definitely a case for a last resort.'

'Yeah...' Alex scratched the back of his neck. 'Having to tell the institute their rep had been eaten wouldn't have done your application any good.' He flashed an apologetic smile at Anna.

'That's assuming I'd lived to tell them anything,' Jack said, emulating Alex's bantering tone.

He wasn't about to let on how he felt about failing to protect Anna. He glanced across at her, noting the pallor under her tan and the tremor in her hand as she pulled it across her forehead. She knew precisely how dangerous their situation had been, but he wondered if she'd guessed that his concentration had lapsed.

'Thanks, Alex.' He clapped the other man on the shoulder. 'Excellent foresight and quick thinking. I was...distracted for a moment.'

Alex shook his head. 'Even if you hadn't been,

I don't think you'd have heard him or seen him coming. Just a case of wrong time, wrong place.'

'Maybe.' Jack half turned towards Anna. 'You okay to walk on? Or I could call up the lodge on the radio and have someone come to get us.'

He saw indecision fighting with stubbornness in her expression. She looked across the bush in the direction the lion had taken and then back at him. 'It was my choice to come. I'll be okay,' she said, her voice quiet.

Jack glanced at his watch. 'We should just make it back before dark if we don't have any more unexpected encounters. Let's go.'

Feeling nervous in the bush was an unfamiliar experience for Anna, and she didn't like it at all. If she'd thought about it, she would have assumed it would simply never be a problem for her. Her confidence, built over the years by a combination of experience and expert guidance, had always been rock-solid. Like being able to ride a bicycle or swim, it had been something she could always rely on. But now her eyes searched the scrub in the thickening dusk, her senses primed to spot the gleam of an eye or a rustle in the undergrowth.

She walked between the two men, glad to have their solid protection on either side. Her shoulder bumped against Jack's arm and her fingers brushed his, but he made no attempt to take her hand or offer reassurance. She told herself she was relieved. She wouldn't have wanted him to discover her palm slick with the sweat of fear. She wiped her hands against the back of her jeans, and tried to keep her breath from stopping in her throat when an owl on an early-evening hunt swooped over their heads with a sudden quiet rush of wings, and a hippo snorted loudly in the riverbed below.

When the lights of the lodge flickered through the dusk as they rounded a bend in the track she breathed more easily. Within a few steps they had crossed the causeway, with its sluggish trickle of water beneath, and hopped over the cattle grid into the safety of the compound. At the foot of the steps onto the deck Jack and Alex paused. Anna kept going.

'Anna?' Jack called. 'I'll be with you in a minute. Alex and I...'

'It's okay.' She glanced back at him. 'I need to write up my notes. And anyway, the jet-lag...'

He caught up with her as she made her way along the path towards her suite. The solar lanterns were flickering into life and Venus hung, diamond-bright, in the violet sky. He fell into step beside her, walking in silence.

At her door, she dug in her pocket for the key and turned to face him. 'Jack, I'm tired and I have to work. If you don't mind...'

He raised a hand towards her but let it fall to his

side. 'I put you in danger. I let my guard down, and I'm sorry. If anything had happened to you...'

Anna shook her head and looked away, avoiding his eyes. 'Like Alex said, it was a case of wrong time, wrong place. You couldn't have predicted it. It's the kind of thing that goes with the territory. I knew... I *know* that.'

'Even so, I allowed myself to be distracted and that's unforgiveable. We were lucky to get a second chance after a mistake like that.'

'Well, I'm glad it was you and me and not one of the guests.' She slanted a look up at him. 'Although one of them *was* the reason we were there in the first place.'

Jack bit his lip. 'It seems protecting you is built into my soul, Anna. It's what I've always done.'

'Almost always, Jack. And, like I said, I'm all grown up now. I can look after myself.'

'Almost?' Jack stared at her. 'When have I ever not? Until today?'

'Sending me off to England against my will felt like the withdrawal of your protection. It was terrifying.'

Jack took a step back. 'Some time,' he growled, 'if you'll agree to listen, I'll explain to you how that was actually for your own protection.' He pushed his fingers through his hair. 'I need to go.'

He turned on his heel, but stopped and looked back at her.

Anna raised her eyebrows at him.

'Were you afraid this evening?' he asked.

Anna considered the question for no longer than a moment. 'I was. And acknowledging it was a shock, because I've never been afraid in the bush. And my fear was compounded.'

'How?' He turned back to her, intrigued.

She laughed softly. 'I was terrified the lion would attack, but I was almost more terrified that you'd shoot him. I didn't want to be the reason for a last resort shot.'

'You're still remarkable, Anna. Do you know that?'

He reached across the space between them, but she snapped her head back, out of his reach.

'You and I need to put some space between us, Jack.' She unlocked the door. 'Physical and emotional space. Goodnight.'

'Then I'll see you tomorrow,' he said, as she pulled the door closed behind her.

Jack re-joined the path and picked up his pace as he made his way to his quarters. He felt wrong-footed and dissatisfied with the way things had played out, and not only because he blamed himself for putting Anna in danger.

He rephrased that thought. He was beating himself up for allowing his possessive jealousy to put her in danger. He had no claim on her. He'd relinquished that eleven years ago. And he couldn't dictate how she spent these few short days at Themba. He needed her experience at the lodge to be as positive as possible to ensure their best shot at getting funding, he told himself. She had a job to do and he had to let her do it.

Following her through the door and kissing her senseless wasn't going to happen. Ever. Again. She'd made that crystal-clear this morning. What annoyed him—okay, *hurt* him, if he was being honest—was how she seemed to be fine with it, while his unreliable body told him he most definitely was not.

But one good thing had come out of their meeting with the big cat. If she'd been afraid perhaps she'd respect the rules of Themba and not go wandering off too far for her safety and too close to crocodiles. He rolled his shoulders and tried to relax. She'd caused him enough anxiety in the past to last him a lifetime.

Anna leaned back against the closed door and pressed her palms flat onto its surface. It felt solid and reassuring and she breathed a long sigh of relief. The encounter with the lion had shaken her, and more than anything she'd wanted to pull Jack through this door, bury her face in his broad, hard chest and feel the strength of his arms around her…hear his deep voice telling her everything was okay.

But then everything would most definitely *not* have been okay. Because it wouldn't have stopped there. She knew that, and she knew it couldn't happen.

That kiss last evening had taken her to the brink of her self-control. Her white-hot reaction to Jack had shocked and unsettled her. She'd felt in control until the moment his lips had touched hers, but after that nothing had made sense. As a love-struck teenager she'd fantasised about kissing him, being in his arms and feeling his hands caress her, but after that the picture had gone fuzzy. Her naïve imagination hadn't quite known where to go from there.

She knew where she wanted to go now. She glanced at the inviting bed.

But he hadn't followed her through the door.

She tried to quell the small curl of disappointment and pulled a bottle of iced water from the fridge. She rolled its cool contours, frosted with condensation, across her forehead and walked over to the glass doors, but she didn't open them. She felt shaky and vulnerable, and not strong enough to deal with any posturing over-confident monkeys.

She'd believed she could handle Jack. She'd never dreamed for a moment that handling herself would be so difficult. Because in eleven years she'd never met a man she couldn't walk away from. This raw, dangerous attraction which smouldered between them was outside her experience. One tiny spark of encouragement would ignite it, and once lit she knew it would consume them both in red-hot flames of need.

And then what?

It would be impossible to do her job here. She'd lose her professional credibility and the respect of her colleagues.

When a niggling voice of doubt asked her if she'd cared if that meant she could stay at Themba with Jack, she crushed it with the ruthless disdain it deserved. Once she'd wanted this life, but her aspirations had changed. Nothing she wanted now was to be found among the dust and fever trees of Themba. A secure home, a husband, a family—those were the things she'd made her goal and they did not exist here.

And Jack had obviously been deadly serious when he'd tossed those crushing words at her over his shoulder all those years ago. *'I don't want a wife. Not ever.'* If he'd wanted one, he would have found a wife by now.

Anna cracked the seal of the bottle and swallowed three deep gulps of water. She wiped her hand across her face and rested her forehead against the cool glass of the terrace doors. Jack only needed her here to back up his application for funding, nothing more. To give in to this force that sucked them towards each other would be madness.

Her own personal reasons for being here were different. He'd dismissed her from his life, and now she'd returned to show him she didn't need him. At all.

It was just going to be a lot more complicated than she'd thought...

Showered and changed, and only five minutes late, Jack climbed the steps to the Marula Restaurant two at a time. The adrenalin from the evening's encounter had ebbed, but its effect still pulsed in his veins. He felt as if he was running on empty...running away from the searing temptation that had gripped him outside Anna's door.

She'd been afraid and he was to blame. He'd apologised, but he'd wanted to express it in more than plain words. She hadn't let him.

He paused under the arch of the entrance to the restaurant and glanced around. The visitors were all there, most of them deep in earnest discussion. He hung back for a moment, steadying himself with a deep breath and telling himself that the evening would soon be over and they'd all be gone tomorrow.

Usually he relished these visits from intelligent and committed academics. They offered an opportunity for the exchange of ideas and informed discussion about the environmental, zoological and humanitarian problems which beset the planet and how they impacted specifically on his vision for Themba. He valued outside opinion and fresh perspectives.

But Anna's arrival yesterday had felt like a bomb exploding in his life, and now he just wanted them gone. He needed to devote his energy to unravelling the tangle of emotions her sudden appearance had dragged to the surface of his consciousness. And he needed to find a way to stop the overwhelming physical need her presence had unleashed.

With sharp clarity he remembered her sliding out of the old Land Rover Defender at the beginning of the school holidays, when she was fifteen and he was twenty three. His breath had caught somewhere in his chest as those going-on-for-ever legs had appeared, followed by a lithe body and then her face, split by a delighted grin at seeing him, her slightly tilted eyes shining as she tugged the toggle off the end of her schoolgirl plait and unravelled her gold-streaked hair down to her waist.

Suddenly his perception of her had shifted slightly. To put his arms around her and give her the hug she'd expected as she'd flung herself at him felt inappropriate. So he'd dipped his head and embraced her stiffly, pulling away much too quickly.

This was Anna, and she trusted him to protect her as he'd always done. Recognising that she was growing up was difficult.

Yesterday, she had pulled away...

Dan stepped up to him. 'Everything okay?'

He nodded. 'Everything's great, thanks.'

He looked beyond Dan and saw that all faces were turned towards him and the silence was loaded with expectation.

'We heard there was a lion. Everyone heard the shot.' Dan dropped his voice. 'What happened, Jack?'

Hands shoved into his pockets, Jack stepped into the pool of light cast by the lanterns which hung in the branches above them. 'Yes, you heard right.' He made sure his voice was loud enough for everyone to hear. 'There was a lion. A fully-grown male and a beautiful specimen. I would guess he weighed upwards of five hundred and fifty pounds.' He shrugged. 'We were in his territory and he wasn't pleased to see us. But...' he paused, looking out into the darkness beyond the tables, which were set with traditionally patterned cloths, earthenware and chunky blown glass '...at Themba our policy is only ever to shoot an animal as an absolute last resort. One of our trackers, Alex, fired over the lion's head, startling him. He retreated into the safety of the ravine and we walked home.'

Dan's eyes were still on him, and the unspoken question in them had not gone away. He knew what the question was. It concerned his integrity and his ability to make a split-second decision. But he didn't know the answer to it and that annoyed the hell out of him.

'*What?*' he demanded.

Dan lifted his shoulders a fraction, his look unwavering. 'Nothing, Jack. Nothing at all.'

Jack pulled his hands from his pockets and stepped forward. 'Now, does everyone have a drink?'

Much later, Jack paused on the path outside Anna's suite. He was relieved to see it was in darkness. It made not knocking on the door a whole lot easier.

He imagined her asleep in the wide bed, those long legs tangled in the rumpled bedclothes, her hair spread like cloth of gold across the pillow, and he swore. Yes, she was all grown up and she no longer needed his protection, but accepting that truth was as difficult as hell. He'd been shocked rigid by a blinding realisation as he'd faced that lion. Anna remained as precious to him today as when she'd emerged from the chrysalis of that bright blanket twenty-seven years ago. That was why the question he'd seen in Dan's eyes, and which had been hammering in his brain all evening, was so scary.

If the lion hadn't been startled by Alex's shout and carefully judged shot, what would have happened? Would there have been enough time for him to squeeze the trigger, as the other man had calculated?

But that wasn't really the question... He scuffed the toe of his suede boot in the gravel. The real question was, would his shot have found its mark at all even if he had fired?

Everyone knew that the last time he'd been required to shoot an animal as a last resort he'd failed.

And the guilt of that failure would haunt him for the rest of his life.

CHAPTER FIVE

'I THOUGHT,' SAID ANNA, as Jack swung the Land Rover off the road onto a dusty patch of earth, 'we were going to visit the school.'

'We are.' He pulled up the handbrake and killed the engine.

'The sign above that door says *Clinic*.'

He looked towards the brick-built building in front of them. A group of women standing in the sun, babies on their hips, turned their heads in their direction. One of them lifted a hand in greeting.

'When we built the school five years ago I decided to incorporate a clinic. Parents bringing their children to school can see a doctor or a nurse at the same time, if necessary.' He released his seat belt and shouldered the door open. 'Some parents walk their children miles to school each day. This arrangement saves them unnecessary journeys.'

He slammed the driver's door and walked around to open Anna's.

'The clinic isn't staffed every day, but there is a fairly reliable schedule. A rota of doctors and health visitors are here three times a week. The system works...mostly.'

Anna slid out of her seat and pulled a straw hat onto her head. As they rounded the end of the building a dusty playground behind a low wall came into view. A spreading marula tree cast a wide pool of shade in the middle of it.

She stopped, getting her bearings. 'Wasn't the school under this tree?'

Jack nodded. 'It was. It's where I had my first proper lessons, and later so did you.'

She strolled to the tree and put a hand on its trunk, running her palm over the bark. 'Joseph used to walk with us, teaching us bushcraft on the way, and you always gave me a piggyback ride when I got tired. It seemed like miles, but it wasn't far at all.'

'It was too far for a five-year-old's legs.' His gaze dropped to her denim-clad thighs then flicked away. 'Come on, they're expecting us in Class One.'

Half an hour later they left a sea of waving hands and a chorus of farewells behind them. Anna shook her head as they climbed back into the vehicle. 'This is a great project, Jack. I'm very impressed.'

'Are you really?' he asked. 'And with the clinic?'

'Really. This has been achieved in…what… five years?'

'Yeah.' He nodded. 'It wasn't without its difficulties, but the payback is immense. Education is the key to so many problems. It's the route out of poverty for these rural communities.'

His tone was passionate. She looked across at him as he turned the key in the ignition. His mouth was set in a straight, strong line and his expression was sober. The engine settled into a steady rhythm and he adjusted the air-conditioning.

'This one school and clinic must have improved the lives of so many people, adults and children, and it's all thanks to you. That must feel amazing.'

'No, not amazing—although I'm pleased, obviously. It's the teachers and healthcare workers who are amazing, and the kids who walk for miles each day to come to school. I'm counting on the knock-on effects of education filtering through to a reduction in poaching. But as long as a gram of rhino horn fetches more on the market than a gram of cocaine it'll be a battle.'

'Is that really true?'

'Apparently. Although I don't know the current value of either. What I do know is that the life of these communities depends on the ecology. Without the wildlife there would be no tourism, and many livelihoods would collapse. Our aim is to provide education, so that more people can be employed locally in tourism and research. We support the establishment of small businesses, too.'

'Could we visit some of those? Last evening Alice told me about the one her mother has set up. The more positive examples of enterprise I can include in my findings, the better your chance of success in getting funds.'

'Of course. I'll arrange some meetings.'

'Some of the funding you're applying for will go towards extending the school and the research centre, right?'

'Absolutely. A bigger school means more pupils and more teachers. An enhanced research centre means more local jobs and an increased understanding of the perilous existence of some of our most endangered species, as well as finding ways their decline can be stopped, or at least slowed.'

Anna was silent for a moment. Then she bent her head and rubbed at a patch of dust on her jeans. 'This is what drives you, Jack. Isn't it?' She gestured towards the school building. 'Before, it was your work at the mine, but now it's all this.'

Jack leaned forward and rested his forearms on the top of the steering wheel, staring straight ahead. 'We all know about climate change and how we're wrecking the planet, with our plastics, our logging and extraction and burning of fossil fuels, but most of us think there's nothing we can do about it. If we all did something, however small, it would…it *will*…make a difference.' He turned his head towards her. 'In a city like London you're removed from it. Here, I can *see* it happening. The droughts and the floods, the animals disappearing… If we don't do whatever we can to stop it there are species that *your* children will never see. I cannot—*will* not—stand by and let that happen.' He straightened his arms and pushed himself back into his seat. 'These are the things I can do. It may not be enough, and it may be too late, but doing nothing is not an option.'

The determination radiating from him was so forceful that Anna almost felt intimidated. He was fixed on a difficult path and it was obvious nothing was going to distract him from his goals.

She frowned. 'What will you do if your application is turned down? Will you find another way?'

Jack beat a rhythm on the steering wheel with his fingers. 'I'll be disappointed. But it's not so much about the financial support as the recognition we'd receive if your institute endorses us. Internationally the profile of Themba and the work we're doing would be raised, and that would be much more valuable.'

'Your ambitions are admirable, Jack, and your achievements remarkable. But there is one thing that puzzles me…' She shuffled a sheaf of papers on her lap, then tucked them into her leather satchel. 'Eleven years ago, Themba was a collection of thatched huts under the fever trees. There was an outdoor school and no clinic. Most of the able-bodied men went away to work on the mines, and your father existed by entertaining parties of rich big game hunters.'

She kept her eyes on Jack's face and saw his jaw tighten.

His stormy eyes bored into hers. 'Yes.'

'How has all this growth been funded?'

'The diamond mine is hugely profitable.'

Anna nodded. 'Mining is not my field, but the institute will definitely be interested in how it's run, the profit share, and any ethical practices you have in place.' She removed her hat and tossed it onto the back seat, pushing her plait over her shoulder. 'But,' she went on slowly, 'what about the hunting?'

Jack's fingers tightened over the gearstick and an inconvenient memory of those fingers pushing into her hair flared in her brain. His knuckles whitened and she dragged her eyes back up to his face. He was watching her through narrowed eyes.

'No one...*no one*...has paid to shoot an animal on Themba land since the day my father died.'

The atmosphere between them felt charged and unstable. Anna broke their locked stare first and dropped her eyes to his throat. The skin there was smooth and tanned, but a hint of dark hair showed at the neck of his blue-striped shirt. She watched the even rise and fall of his chest and wondered if he'd noticed how her own breathing had grown shallow and quick. She hoped the rapid beat of her pulse was hidden beneath the cotton scarf she wore loosely knotted around her neck.

There seemed to be far more than eleven years between them. The Jack she'd known—her life-long companion and protector—had vanished, and the person sitting only inches from her now felt like a stranger. He was tough, and driven, and she wondered about the circumstances which had shaped him.

She felt a sudden heart-sick longing for that other time, long before he'd sent her away, when they'd been completely at ease with each other... before that treacherous spark of physical aware-ness had flickered to life between them. It had smouldered, unattended, for all the years they'd been apart, and now it had swelled into a flame that threatened to roar out of control.

Anna forced herself to suck in a deeper breath. 'I believe you, Jack.' Despite the cold air pumping into the vehicle through the air-conditioning vents she felt her cheeks heat under his stare. 'And... and I was sorry to hear about your father's death.' She reached out and put a hand on his shoulder but he shrugged it off.

'Thanks.' Jack nodded once. 'Not many peo-ple mourned him. And the hunters wasted no time moving on to other establishments when I banned them from Themba. My father had become a liability—a danger to himself and others.'

He stamped on the clutch and engaged the gears as if to close the subject.

'The visitors left this morning, so I'm free for a few days until the next party arrives.' He spun the wheel and turned onto the dusty road. 'Perhaps you'd like to join me for dinner this evening, so we can continue this discussion. I can provide any information you need on the mining operation.'

Jack knocked on Anna's door and waited. A breeze rustled in the trees overhead and he frowned. The flare of anxiety which had lain dormant and which he associated with looking after Anna unfurled in his chest. *Where was she?* But before his imagination could run wild, down into the riverbed amongst the crocs, or up onto the rocky outcrop where he'd heard the rasping cough of a leopard earlier, the door opened.

Each time he saw Anna he had to fight to control his response, to douse the fire which burned through his veins. The reality of her presence packed far more punch than the thought of her. And God knew his thoughts were hot enough.

Because he was sure they were clearly expressed in his eyes, he pushed his hands into the pockets of his jeans and ducked his head. But when he lifted it again his gaze tracked up her legs, and up some more...

Stop it. Now.

He took in the black skinny jeans...the loose top in a colour which was neither blue nor green and yet the most intense hue of both. The breeze which had shivered through the treetops a moment ago swooped down to earth and unhelpfully flattened the shimmering fabric against her body, sculpting her curves in silk.

'Hi.' She threw him a cool smile. She'd freed her hair from its plait and it flowed in waves down her back from the narrow silver band on her head. 'Sorry. I was on the deck, daring the monkeys to come closer.'

'Have you...?' He stopped, reminding himself that she was a responsible adult now.

Her smile widened and his heart turned over.

'Yes, I've closed and locked the glass doors. Can monkeys look disconsolate? I'm sure they did.'

She pulled the door shut behind her and turned the key. Jack stood back as she walked down the path and turned towards the main buildings of the lodge.

'Actually,' he said, managing to pitch his voice at something above a husky growl, 'we're eating at the huts. Since there're no guests for a few days the restaurant is closed. The staff are on duty twenty-four-seven when we're hosting, so it's a chance for them to kick back and recharge a little.'

'Oh…' Anna hesitated. Doubt warred with interest in her expression. 'Okay… It'll be good to see what changes you've made. Although maybe…'

'Maybe?'

She shook her head and the little emerald studs in her ears sparkled with green fire. 'It's just maybe I'd prefer to remember it how it was.'

But she fell into step beside him on the path.

He took her straight to the main living area. She paused on the threshold and looked around, as if trying to match up the space with the one she remembered.

'I can't quite place where I am, Jack.' She shook her head. 'It's all so different.'

'I'll take you on a tour and explain.' He nodded towards a door. 'This way.'

Ten minutes later they were back in the living area. Anna slid open the glass doors and walked out across the deck.

Wooden chairs with deep rust-coloured canvas cushions furnished the space. The view over the river was dissolving in the soft evening light.

Jack watched her turn and walk towards him. He ached to turn back the clock, to an easier time when they'd been friends, and close, and life had been less complicated. But he closed down that avenue of thought with an irritated shake of his head. They'd both moved on. There could be no going back.

'Drink?' he asked.

'Yes, please. Could it be a glass of that Sauvignon Blanc I had the night I arrived?'

'It could be.'

He pulled a bottle from the small bar fridge and twisted a corkscrew into the top. When he looked up again Anna was standing in front of the framed photo of his mother. He picked up the two glasses of wine and held one out to her.

'Is this your mother, Jack?' Her fingers closed around the glass stem and she raised the goblet in a half-salute.

Jack took the time to swallow a mouthful of wine before answering. 'Yes. That was taken about a year before she died.'

Anna's eyes went back to the picture. 'She's very beautiful. I don't remember seeing that picture before.'

'After she died my father refused to have any pictures of her in the house.' He shrugged. 'That was the one I managed to save. I hid it.'

Anna's eyes filled with sympathy. 'I'm sorry. She was never a part of my life here, but you must have missed her terribly.'

Jack nodded. 'Yeah. It was a long time ago, but sometimes I still wonder…'

'What?'

He took another swallow of wine. 'How life

would have been if she hadn't died. But it's no use speculating.'

'I'm glad you saved her picture. I wish I had one of my parents. I have no idea what either of them looked like. George knew my grand-parents, and apparently they were so upset when my mother gave up her life in London to follow my father to Africa they cut all ties with her and destroyed all the family pictures.' She shook her head. 'Seems a bit extreme, don't you think?'

'That depends. I destroyed a lot of family me-mentoes when my father died.' He kept his back to her. 'But they were mostly hunting trophies and pictures of macho men standing on the ani-mals they'd shot for sport. I'd always hated them.'

'The men or the pictures?'

'Both.'

'I hated them too, once I was old enough to un-derstand who they were and what they did. And the photos…they were awful.'

Jack inclined his head towards the glass doors and Anna followed him onto the deck.

'There,' she said, 'is where the hammock used to be.'

He nodded. 'I had the deck built around the trunks of those two trees. They give excellent shade in the afternoon.' He steered the conversa-tion away from the hammock. 'Burning all those photographs was one of the first things I did after my father died.'

They settled into chairs, facing the river and the darkening hills beyond it. Anna slipped her feet out of her flat pumps and tucked her legs underneath her. Jack swallowed and gripped the stem of his wine glass between his fingers.

He'd caught a glimpse of her smooth thigh beneath her bathrobe two nights ago, and the memory of it snagged at him repeatedly. How would that satin skin feel under his slightly roughened fingertips? And how would he feel if he could trace a path further up, towards her forbidden and secret places?

He leaned forward and propped his elbows on his knees.

'But he was your father, Jack. Surely you took time to grieve for him?'

'My grief was for the man he should have been. The one my mother must have thought she married. By the time he died alcohol was his only pleasure, and I don't think that even took the edge off the guilt he felt. He was tormented by her loss, and the part he'd played in it.'

He'd kept his eyes trained on the horizon, but he knew Anna's were fixed on him.

'You never talked about her, Jack.'

'No. After she died no one was allowed to mention her name, and after a while not talking about her became the norm. My father tried to erase all evidence of her existence from Themba—and he succeeded to a certain degree. But I suspect it wasn't so easy to wipe his memory.'

'You told me once that your mother died of a cerebral haemorrhage while your father was away…' Anna wrapped her arms around her shins and rested her chin on her knees. 'But you never wanted to talk about it.'

'No,' Jack repeated.

He put his glass down on the deck and folded his arms across his chest. The familiar sense of panic threatened to impede his breath as his heart rate picked up. But he'd learned to control it years ago, like he controlled everything else in his life. By sheer will power. The guilt was a different thing altogether. It could hit him when he least expected it, and it felt like being kicked in the chest by a buffalo. It made him gasp for air.

'I never have talked about it because the guilt is…crippling.'

'Guilt? But it wasn't your fault. Not any of it.'

'When my father left that day to go hunting he told me to look after my mother. I felt proud that he thought I was old enough. Afterwards I knew it was because he felt guilty about leaving her when she was ill. She had a terrible headache and begged him not to go. I couldn't save her. I failed. She was my responsibility and I let her down—and my father, too.'

He dragged his eyes from where they'd been scanning the darkness beyond and found her steady gaze fixed on him. When she spoke her voice was gentle, and more like the voice he remembered.

'It must have been terrifying for you. I'm so sorry.' She extended a hand towards him, but then dropped it into her lap.

He shook his head and wiped a hand across his face. 'It was how my father behaved when he returned that was frightening. He smashed things up and threatened the people who'd tried to help her. Then he went on a bender. And when he eventually sobered up, days later, he was like a different person. Hunted instead of hunter.'

'It wasn't your fault,' Anna repeated.

The night had fallen swiftly, but the glow of the solar lanterns on the deck kept the dark at bay. Jack pushed himself back in his chair and tipped his head to look at the emerging stars. His logical brain told him that Anna was right. He knew there was nothing his eight-year-old self could have done. But as a child he hadn't understood that.

And then there was that other guilt, which he could never reveal to her.

It was true that he'd feared for her safety at the hands of the rough groups of men who'd come to Themba to hunt. He could tell her that. But had he used them as a convenient excuse?

Because the real reason he'd sent her away had been his fear of his own feelings. He'd feared that the hot surge of desire that took over his body every time he saw her would be the one thing he wouldn't be able to control. It made him vulnerable to hurt. And he'd decided a long time before that nobody would ever hurt him again. So he'd hurt Anna, instead.

Jack closed his eyes briefly, then stood up. 'Let's go in. I'll get the food.'

Anna sat still, mulling over Jack's words.

Perhaps now she could understand a little of his father's behaviour. As she'd grown up she'd wondered what had made him assume responsibility for an orphaned two-year-old.

She knew it had taken him months to establish that the people who'd died in the plane crash were her parents, Aidan Jones and Rebecca Kendall. The flight appeared to have had no origin and no destination and it was many more months before accident investigation officials let him know its probable point of departure. By then the state, further north, where they'd lived, was in the grip of a vicious civil war and many government buildings had been destroyed. Public records had been burned and no wills or birth certificates had survived. He registered Anna's existence and address with the Consul in Cape Town and let her stay at Themba.

And then, when she was five, a letter had arrived from Dr George Lane. Although he did not expect to hear from Rebecca often, he wrote, when she'd been silent for almost three years he'd grown concerned. He'd written to several Consuls to ask for help tracing her. The one in Cape Town had given him his answer.

All George had was a letter from Rebecca telling him of Anna's birth and asking him to look after her if necessary. She hoped she could grow up in Africa but would like her to complete her education in England.

Once, in an attempt to engage with him, Anna had asked Jack's father why he'd allowed her to remain at Themba. He'd stared at her for a long time, and then switched his gaze to the massive baobab tree in a far corner of the compound.

'I had to make atonement.' His voice had roughened. 'I'm afraid of failing another human being.'

Now she walked back into the open-plan living area, where a lamplit table had been set with a bowl of pasta smothered in a creamy sauce, a salad of green leaves and places for two.

'Mmm... Smells delicious. Thank you.'

Jack topped up her wine glass as she sat down.

'At last,' she said, 'I think I understand your father's motivation.'

'For what?'

'I asked him once why he'd let me stay and he said he had to make atonement. That he was afraid of failing another human being.'

Jack propped his forearms on the table and

looked across at her. 'Who do you believe he was afraid of failing?' He frowned. 'You or me?'

'Well…at the time I didn't understand him. I didn't know what atonement meant. But now I think he meant me. He'd failed your mother, but he'd taken me in. Perhaps somehow in his mind he thought he'd balanced the scales.'

'He also knew that you'd become very important to me—very quickly. Giving you up would have meant him taking you from me, when I'd already lost my mother.'

Anna nodded slowly. 'Perhaps it was for both of us, then. I hadn't considered that.'

'I was always desperately afraid that something would happen to you, or you'd be taken away.' Jack leaned back and folded his arms. 'I made keeping you safe my purpose in life. I hadn't been able to save my mother, and my father had become a distant, isolated figure, but I was determined to stop anything bad from happening to you. Ever.' His eyelids dropped briefly. 'That's why, when you were eighteen…' He shook his head and then brought a fist down onto the table—hard. 'God, I hated those men.'

Anna jumped, startled. 'What men? You're not making sense, Jack.'

'The men who made me send you away.'

'It was *you* who sent me away, Jack. Three weeks early. You said you'd explain why, and that it was for my own safety, if I'd listen.' She cupped a hand under her chin. 'Maybe now's the time?'

'Well, it wasn't because I thought you'd become over-confident in the bush—although you'd caused me to panic more than once.'

'I thought it was because I'd asked...okay, *begged* you to marry me, Jack. Your father wanted you to find a wife and I saw myself as the obvious solution. The thought of leaving Themba terrified me. Everything I knew was here. Everything I...loved.' She picked up her glass and swirled the pale wine. 'Even though I knew it was my mother's wish, the pain has never quite gone away.'

Jack looked exhausted, and sad, and Anna wanted nothing more than to walk around the table and put her arms around his shoulders, rest her cheek on his head. But she had a good idea of where that would lead, and she wasn't going there. She was here to do a job and she'd do it professionally, as well as she could. And then she'd walk away. Show Jack that she'd grown out of him and into a much bigger life, where she could fulfil her dream of having a home and a family of her own.

Any physical contact between them, even a simple gesture of comfort, would be the quickest route to crossing the boundaries they'd set. His comment earlier in the day about her future children—he obviously never planned to have any—and now seeing his home was all the proof she needed that Jack had no plans to allow a woman into his life.

From the leather furniture to the dark wooden shelves packed with books and the slate-tiled floors, this house was a private male sanctuary. The wide bed in his bedroom, with its pale grey linen and quilt, had pillows on one side only. The chrome and grey marble wet room had a glass door onto a secluded part of the deck where he'd installed an outdoor shower.

As she'd walked back into the living room, its single note of femininity had hit her between the eyes. The picture of his mother. It was in stark contrast to the ambience of virile masculinity surrounding it.

'I know I hurt you, but I had to make you leave,' he said now.

'I figured that much out, but I thought it was because my marriage proposal had embarrassed you. Was there some other reason?'

'I had to make you leave because of the discussion a party of hunters had had around the firepit a couple of nights before. It concerned you—although I'd rather not go into the details of their observations. Then they started placing bets on which one of them could get you into bed first. From their language it was obvious they didn't have romantic seduction in mind, and that it wouldn't matter if no actual bed was involved.'

Anna felt as if the air had thickened and something heavy was compressing her chest. How naïve had she been? As Jack had pointed out, her experience of life had been bounded by Themba and a girls' boarding school. The possibility that any of those blustering, sweaty old men would consider her as anything other than a girl wouldn't have occurred to her in a million years.

She felt slightly sick.

'I was always uncomfortable around those men. I tried to keep out of sight as much as possible. I…I didn't think they'd even noticed me.'

'I think that was part of it,' Jack said. 'Your elusiveness made the chase more exciting.'

'So,' Anna said, 'when you said I had to leave it wasn't to save me from a rogue elephant or a bad-tempered rhino.' She swallowed. 'Or marriage to you.'

'It wasn't. And I don't want a wife.'

'Yes, I remember.' She nodded. 'Not ever. Why was your father so insistent that you find one?'

Jack laid his fork on the side of his plate. 'He was goading me. We were arguing about everything by then. I wanted the hunting to stop, so we could turn Themba into a model game reserve where important research could be undertaken. I wanted to be at the forefront of the fight against poaching.' In a gesture of frustration he raked his fingers through his hair. 'I told him I'd never marry after I'd seen the sort of life a wife could expect at Themba, and his response was that he'd consider some of the reforms if I found a wife.'

'I would have thought you were crazy if you'd tried to explain to me about those men,' said Anna.

'I did write to you to explain. Several times.'

'I destroyed your letters without opening them. I was hurt and humiliated, and for a long time I told myself I'd never come back.'

Anna remembered the arrival of each letter. Every time George had left one on her desk its presence had stolen her attention and sapped her concentration until she had picked it up between thumb and forefinger, carried it downstairs and dropped it into the drawing room fire. Luckily the letters had stopped by the time spring came and the fire was no longer lit.

'But you did come back. And I'm glad. Because there's something I need to show you.'

Jack pulled the battered backpack from a high shelf in his dressing room. He wiped some of the dust off it with his sleeve, then carried it into the living room and dumped it on the glass coffee table.

'That's your school backpack.'

Anna had come to stand next to him, but he sat down on the leather sofa and patted the space beside him.

'Yeah, it is. Sit down, Anna.'

She perched on the edge of the seat and he noticed the healthy gap she'd left between them. She wasn't crossing boundaries, either.

He tugged at the zipper of the bag and pulled out a bundle wrapped in a blanket, its pattern dulled with age. He unrolled it on the table.

'You were wearing these when you were brought to Themba.'

The tee shirt had faded to the palest pink, and all that remained of the elephant on the front was a faint outline. Anna stared at it and he saw her throat tighten.

'That was mine?'

He nodded. 'Yes. And these.'

The colours of the candy-striped dungarees had lasted better. They had a pocket in the bib and two slanting pockets at the sides. The brass buttons and buckles still had a dull shine.

She put out a hand and fingered the fabric. 'And I was wearing them... My mother must have chosen these clothes to dress me in on that last morning.'

He saw her teeth fasten on her bottom lip as a tremor ran through her.

'You were bundled up in this blanket and the women unwrapped you like a parcel on what passed for our kitchen table.' He tipped his head. 'Out there—beyond where the kitchen is now. To me it seemed like a miracle as this fairy child with candyfloss hair and eyes the colour of my favourite green marble emerged from the folds of a rough blanket. They undressed you to give you a wash.'

Anna picked up the tee shirt and spread it on her knees, tracing around the outline of the elephant. 'I can't believe I was ever this tiny.' She laughed, but the sound caught in her throat.

'You didn't want to be washed. You demanded that I pick you up and then you hung on to me like a meerkat. They had to prise you out of my arms."

'But where have these clothes been all this time?'

'When I began renovating the huts I found them at the back of a cupboard. What was in the pockets was more interesting, though.'

Jack undid the buckle which fastened a flap over an outside pouch of the backpack and pulled out a cloth bag. The contents rattled as he tipped them onto the table.

There was a long, charged silence. Anna left the tee shirt on her knees and leaned forward, peering at the chunks of rock. She ran a finger over their four-sided shapes. They looked like pale lumps of glass.

'Rough diamonds…' He could barely hear her voice.

'They were sewn into the pockets of your dungarees. Evidently in the excitement of your arrival nobody noticed your clothes were heavier than they should have been.'

He picked up one of the stones and rolled it around in his palm.

Anna's breathing was quick in the quiet room. She lifted her eyes to meet his and then looked back at the stones.

'I don't know what to do with them. Is it even legal to own them? And where did they come from?'

He held up a hand. 'Slow down, Anna. What you do with them is your decision. They could be worth a lot of money, but they might be difficult to sell because there's no Kimberley Process Certificate to prove they were ethically mined— I'm guessing they were not. As for where they came from…it could probably be established, but the answer might not be what you want to hear.'

'What do you mean?'

'I've done some research and found out a bit about your father.'

Anna's hand shot out and her fingers circled Jack's wrist.

'What have you discovered?'

'It's not much.' He took her hand and placed it on the sofa between them. 'The plane you were in wasn't his. It had been stolen a couple of weeks earlier from somewhere north of here. There's no evidence pointing to your father as the thief, but he was probably working for the man who was. There was a story circulating that your father and his accomplice had found a valuable seam of diamond rock and kept its location a secret. He was probably taking some of the gems—these diamonds—as proof of the find, to show to someone they hoped would finance an illicit mining operation.'

Jack watched a series of emotions flit across Anna's features. She wiped at her cheeks with the heel of her hand and crossed her arms across her body. The sleek academic who had climbed those steps two days earlier and extended her cool hand towards him had vanished. She looked shaken, and vulnerable, and suddenly very young, and at last Jack recognised something of the Anna he remembered.

He ached to take her in his arms to comfort her, but he didn't dare. It would be far too dangerous.

Anna twisted to face him. 'This is the closest... the *nearest* I've ever been able to get to my parents or to who I am, Jack.' She glanced down at the faded clothes and the diamonds. 'It means more to me than I can say that you kept these.'

She bit her lip and balled her fists in her lap.

'Don't do that.'

'What?'

Jack raised a hand and ran his thumb along her bottom lip. 'Don't bite your lip. You'll hurt yourself.'

'Oh...' She turned her face into his palm. 'I

didn't realise. There's too much to think about and it's overwhelming.'

Jack took a steadying breath as his fingers came into contact with the soft skin of her cheek. His hand slid around the back of her head and their eyes locked.

'Anna…' he said on a breath.

'Mmm…'

He lost the battle with his willpower as she dropped her forehead to his shoulder and he pulled her into a hug. He thought of how it had felt to have her pressed against him while he squinted down the barrel of the rifle at the lion. He remembered the question in Dan's eyes and wondered how he could have doubted he would have pulled the trigger in time.

There was no lion this time. No gun. Just the two of them. Alone in his house, where nobody would find them and her research report would not be compromised. She was shaken, and her emotions were running high, and he'd never take advantage of that, but he had to comfort her. Nothing more.

For a brief second he rested his cheek on the crown of her head, and then he settled her into his arms.

'I wish,' he said, 'that I could tell you more.'

He felt the slight movement of her head against his shoulder as she tipped her face up towards him. A convulsive shiver shook her and he tightened his arms around her.

'You've given me a link to them,' she said. 'Something tangible. I didn't come back expecting to unearth much information about my past. I came...' She shook her head. 'But now I'm thirsty for more—even though there's probably no more to discover. I suppose I've never really come to terms with what happened.'

'I'm so sorry. But if there was more I think I would have found it. Memories have faded, and people are unwilling to talk about anything that might incriminate them even after such a long time.'

Anna rested a hand on his chest and he covered it with his own, rubbing his thumb across her knuckles.

'Seeing these things...suddenly finding a connection to my past...has shaken me. I've wanted to find something...anything...for so long, but it's not only that...'

'What, then?'

'Those men.' She swallowed, her fingers curling and gripping the fabric of his shirt. 'You protected me from them.'

Jack clenched his jaw. 'That was never going to be okay. I knew I couldn't always be here to keep you safe, and I couldn't leave you here, for them...'

As he said the words his conscience wrung

his heart and shame tasted bitter in his mouth.
He was not being honest with her. He'd fought
for weeks to resist Anna's naïve flirtations, and
hearing the hunters discuss her had been the push
he'd needed to send her to England.

If he hadn't, he was afraid he'd have given in.
And that would have made him no better than
one of them.

He looked down. She'd squeezed her eyes shut
but a tear had escaped and trickled across her
cheek. Her body shook with a series of violent
tremors. Somehow, somewhere, he had to find
the strength to resist the tug of his desire.

'You're shocked, Anna. I should have been
more careful about what I told you. You've had
an information overload.'

'Maybe. But I needed to know. I'm all grown
up, Jack.'

That is my biggest problem.

'I just need time to process it,' she went on.

'I'll get you a hot drink. It'll help to calm you
down.' He eased himself away from her. 'Red-
bush tea?'

Anna nodded. 'Thank you.'

Jack stood up.

*And a double whisky for myself, with a cold
shower on the side.*

Anna pressed her knuckles into her eye sockets
and counted through a couple of breaths. *In and*

out. Then she pushed herself off the sofa, testing the reliability of her shaking knees before taking a step through the open glass doors onto the deck.

The temperature had fallen and the cool night air wafted across her face like a balm. Her eyes felt swollen and hot, and an uncontrollable shivering had sapped her energy.

She leaned her elbows on the timber rail and dipped her head. From the fever trees across the narrow river came the distinctive call of an eagle owl. Something mysterious plopped into the sparse water. A mouse, running for cover, scampered through the pool of light thrown by one of the solar lanterns and vanished under the safety of the deck.

She wrestled with her thoughts. Eleven years ago Jack had protected her from the attentions of a lecherous group of men by sending her away. Had he really wanted her to stay? If they could have spent those remaining three weeks together would things have been different between them?

But this evening he'd said those words again. *'I don't want a wife.'*

Pretending it might have been different was a waste of time and emotional energy. Whatever she'd felt for him then had been based on familiarity and the fear of change. His series of revelations this evening had stripped back her emotions until she felt raw and ragged.

Her mind raced. The ghosts of her parents, of

whom she had no memories, no pictures, felt tantalisingly close. Her mother had seemed to speak to her through the small faded garments spread out on the coffee table, and her father through the uncut diamonds. What hopes and dreams, even illegal ones, were bound up in that little collection?

As a child she'd fantasised that their disappearance from her life had all been a mistake and that they'd turn up one day. Perhaps they'd survived, fled the scene of the crash for some reason known only to themselves, and would come back for her so they could be a proper family. In her dreams they'd been strong and good, their flight that fateful day a mercy dash to help someone in need. Even in adulthood she'd clung to the idea that their deaths had been a noble sacrifice.

But now that dream had crumbled like burnt wood into dry ashes. Her childhood clothes looked forlorn, and the illicit diamonds which had led her mother and father to their deaths seemed to radiate a dull malevolence.

She needed time and space to come to terms with this, to recalibrate all of her life up until now. But the effort required seemed too great, and the new narrative she was likely to come up with too painful to confront.

Jack's footsteps sounded on the deck, but she kept her head bowed. He put a mug of tea and a glass on the wide wooden rail beside her, and she stiffened as she felt his hands on her shoulders, easing her round to face him. She'd thought he was going to kiss her again while he'd held her, and she knew she would have let him, but he'd opted to make tea instead.

'Here you are.' Relief laced his voice.

'Where did you expect me to be?' She raised her head.

His thumbs described small circles on her shoulders and he shrugged. Anna caught the gleam of silver in his eyes as he smiled.

'Going on past experience, you could be half a mile away by now, dancing in the moonlight or climbing a tree, so nothing would surprise me.'

'I gave up moonlight dancing and tree-climbing when I left Themba, and I have a healthier respect for the bush now than I did before.'

He nodded. 'Good.' He ran his hands down her arms and linked his fingers with hers. 'How many more days,' he asked, looking over her head into the darkness, 'will it take you to finish your research?'

The beat of her heart seemed to pause, and then it lurched into a quicker, more urgent pattern. She tried not to let her breath stutter. She lifted her chin and turned her head to one side, attempting to think. Her brain was overworked and tired. Too tired to cope with this blindsiding question.

He wanted her gone.

What else could it mean?

He'd told her all he could. Shown her the small collection of her childhood belongings and cleared his conscience. An over-emotional woman trying to make sense of her dubious past would create inconvenient ripples in the smooth fabric of his life and work and take his attention away from the important issues. He needed her to do her research, recommend the funding and then get out of his way.

She was meant to be here for a week, but if she worked long hours she could reduce that time. At least one extra day had been built into the schedule in case of problems, but so far there'd been none. Jack had Themba so well organised and controlled that it had all been straightforward.

One thing was certain, though. Hell would freeze over before she allowed him to tell her she had to leave. She'd go, but she would make it look as if she was going in her own sweet time.

'Um…' She feigned nonchalance, pretending to do a mental calculation. 'I should be leaving on Monday, but everything is so well-documented I can probably complete my investigations before that.'

To her ears her tone sounded a little forced but she hoped Jack wouldn't pick up on it.

'So?'

'So probably two more days? If nothing unexpected turns up I could be gone…' she swallowed '…I could leave on Saturday morning. Friday evening at a push. If there's a daytime flight to Heathrow on Saturday I could catch that.'

'Perfect.' Jack nodded.

He let go of her hands and turned, propping his hips against the railing next to her. Anna caught the smoky whiff of whisky as he lifted a glass containing a hefty measure of amber spirit.

'I'll be able to tell you for sure in the morning.' She cradled the warm mug of tea against her breastbone and bent her head, inhaling the fragrant steam.

'Okay.' Jack sipped at his drink. 'Because the next party of visitors doesn't arrive until Monday, and I'd like to get away for the weekend.'

'Oh?' Anna raised her head and stared straight ahead. 'In that case I'll make sure I'm gone by Friday evening. If you can organise the helicopter pick-up, I'll book into one of the airport hotels.'

'That won't be necessary.'

From the corner of her eye Anna saw him lift the glass to his mouth and swallow.

'I'd like you to come with me.'

Her fingers went rigid and a splash of hot tea sloshed over the rim of her mug. Her head jerked round and she stared at his impassive profile.

'Why?'

'Because I've had an idea. If you agree… If you think it might help you to find closure… I could take you to the site of the plane crash.'

CHAPTER SIX

'ARE YOU OKAY with camping?'

Jack was waiting for her on the deck, at the top of the granite steps. He reached out and gripped the straps of the backpack Anna carried over one shoulder and slid it down her arm.

The question stopped her in her tracks. She'd expected *Did you sleep well?* or *You must be exhausted by the long hours you've worked over the past two days.* Had she really changed that much? Did she look like someone who was not okay with camping?

She considered her reply. In his eyes, she supposed she was a completely different person from the eighteen-year-old he'd dropped at Johannesburg International eleven years ago. He hadn't recognised her when she'd arrived, but she was sure he'd been expecting a man. Not that he'd ever admit to making such a blatantly sexist assumption.

Today, she'd shed her professional academic persona. The slim jeans and white shirt had made way for khaki cargo pants and a *Save the Whales* tee shirt underneath a two-sizes-too-big hoodie. She'd wound an Indian patterned cotton scarf around her neck—mostly for sun protection.

She tucked her hands into the pouch at the front of the hoodie. It was her favourite garment for travelling. On long-haul flights she would pull the hood up, snuggle into it and feel safe and comforted.

Jack had looked away, towards the east, where the sun had recently risen—an orange ball in a wash of soft yellows and pinks, lighting up the few clouds which studded the pale sky. Now she felt his eyes back on her.

For a moment she wondered if she'd spoken the question out loud. *Had* she changed that much? But she saw he was still waiting for an answer.

'I'm fine...absolutely fine with camping, Jack.' She rolled her shoulders and pulled a pair of sunglasses from the pouch. 'I assumed we might not make it there and back in a day, so I'm prepared for a night away.' She glanced at the backpack which Jack had adjusted on his shoulders. 'Perhaps you can show me where we're headed on a map.' She pushed the shades onto the top of her head. 'I like to know where I'm going.'

'Good.' Jack nodded. 'Just thought I'd check because you...' His eyes raked over her and she felt her cheeks warming. 'You're… I thought perhaps camping wouldn't be your thing any more.'

'I may look different, Jack, but I'm the same person underneath.' She looked down at her boots and scuffed the toe of one of them on the wooden deck. She knew that wasn't true. She wasn't the same person at all. 'A grown-up version of the same person,' she amended.

She hadn't camped for years. Okay, not since leaving Themba. But Jack didn't need to know that. All her conservation research and work was connected with the role urban zoos could play in saving critically endangered species. But she wasn't telling Jack that, either. If he really cared he could look her up on the internet and find out for himself in seconds. He probably had.

At the foot of the steps a Land Rover Discovery was parked, painted in camouflage. Anna glanced up at the capsule fitted to the roof.

Jack followed the direction of her gaze as he opened the tailgate and pushed her backpack in, fitting it amongst the camping equipment.

'It's a pop-up tent.' He slammed the door. 'So we don't have to sleep on the ground with one of us waking every couple of hours to stoke the fire to keep nosy animals at bay.'

Anna's mouth dried and she made a conscious effort to stop her jaw from hitting her boots. 'Do we *both* sleep up there? Or will one of us be in the back?'

'There's not a lot of room in the back, unless you sleep curled up. The tent is very comfortable. There's a good mattress. Even I can stretch out on it.'

Was he kidding her?

His expression was serious, his mouth in a straight line, and there was no hint of laughter in his eyes, so she didn't think he was teasing.

Curled up next to him on his sofa two nights ago, and then standing on the deck with her fingers linked in his, all she'd wanted was for him to kiss her. She'd expected it; waited for it. *Ached* for it. But it hadn't happened. He'd been kind and solicitous, making her a cup of tea when the comfort she really sought, the oblivion from the thoughts which caused her head to spin, would have been found in his arms and beneath his mouth. Even though she knew she shouldn't, it was what she'd wanted above all else.

That breath-stealing, body-melting kiss they'd shared the night she arrived had to be a one-off. They'd agreed on that, and Jack was leading the way in sticking to their decision. The avalanche of emotion, memories and regrets it had unleashed had knocked her sideways, because she'd believed she had them firmly under control.

Yet all it had taken was one brush of his lips on hers for that control to be swept away.

Now, sharing a tent with Jack in the bush, miles from anywhere, was going to be the ultimate test for her. But from the look on his face he had no such concerns. Was this trip to be his final deed in wrapping up the problem that was Anna? On Monday he would see her onto the helicopter, breathe a sigh of relief and have forget about her by the time he returned to his office. Another problem solved and filed away.

And yet his memory of their shared past was forensic in its detail. As she climbed into the passenger seat and Jack slammed the door she thought she was more surprised by that than anything else.

Jack unfolded a battered map and spread it out over the console between them. He traced their route with an index finger.

That finger—tapered, strong—and that hand—bronzed and powerful... God, she had to stop fantasising about his palm moving over the contours of her body, those fingers burying themselves in her hair... She dragged her attention back to what he was saying, nailing down a brief fantasy about his mouth along the way.

'We'll leave the made-up road here.' His finger stopped. 'And then follow this track to the north-east. Somewhere around here...' he pointed again '…is a border post, but it won't be manned. It's just a painted sign on a boulder at the side of the track.' He made a circular movement with his fingertip. 'From about here the going will be rough, and the track will disappear completely after a while, but this village—' he tapped the worn print '—is where we're headed. The people who brought you to Themba came from there.'

Anna nodded and snapped the buckle of her seatbelt into place. 'Do you know why?'

'Why?'

'Yes. Why Themba? It's a long way.'

'Yup. Three days' walk back then. There were even fewer roads and tracks than there are now, and a lot more wildlife. But the answer is that they believed there were people at Themba who would know what to do with you. It was the closest, safest option when there wasn't much choice.'

Five hours later, when the gravel road climbed around the shoulder of a hill scattered with giant boulders, Jack pulled the Land Rover over to the side, into the shade of an umbrella thorn, and cut the ignition. Silence settled around them, punctuated by the tick of the cooling motor as the dust drifted away. On the plain below Anna could see a herd of elephant moving through the bush, creating their own small dust cloud.

Jack jumped out of the vehicle and Anna watched him survey their surroundings, studying the rocky slopes above and below and listening intently, before opening the rear door and pulling out a cold box.

'Lunch,' he said. 'I think it's safe to get out.'

Anna swallowed the last mouthful of grilled chicken salad and then bit into the creamy flesh of a peach. Jack twisted the cap off a bottle of water and balanced it on the front bumper between them.

'I thought,' she said, wiping peach juice from her chin, 'the restaurant staff were off duty.'

'They are. I put this together.'

She pushed up the brim of her straw hat and studied his profile. It was achingly familiar, in spite of the years they'd spent apart. Yet it was also subtly different. The serious mouth was bracketed by faint lines. Similar lines radiated from the outer corners of his eyes. Most people would have labelled them laughter lines, but she knew they resulted from years of narrowing his gaze as he squinted into the distance, or the sun.

He tipped his head back and took several deep pulls of water from the bottle in his hand. She watched the smooth bronzed skin of his throat move as he swallowed. The previous version of Jack had scarcely ever set foot in the kitchen. Meals—sometimes at irregular intervals, always plain—had just appeared and been eaten. She'd never given much thought to how they'd got there.

Jack had produced a perfect meal three nights ago and a gourmet picnic today. He was harder, more rugged, but he'd developed skills in the kitchen. And there was that scar...

He turned to face her. 'Have you found what you're looking for?'

Anna swallowed the last mouthful of peach. How did he know she was looking for anything? He'd be the last person she'd share her dreams with. They'd wither and die in the blast of a single one of his scorching glances. She'd learned that the hard way.

'What do you mean?' she managed, when she'd forced some air into her lungs. 'I'm not looking for anything. I'm just...'

'You're staring so hard that I wondered. That's all.'

Ah... She'd been so absorbed in his nearness, in the reality of him, trying to puzzle him out, that she'd read far too much into the question.

'I'm thinking how you're the same yet different,' she said.

'How different?' He raised his eyebrows.

'You're tougher.' She looked away and pressed her hands to the bumper on either side of her hips. 'More...ruthless, somehow.' She smiled, trying to lighten her words. 'Mean and lean.'

'You're right. I am.' He screwed the cap back onto the bottle, tightening it hard. 'I have to be. Getting to where we are now has been a struggle, and the struggle will go on. It's a harsh environment and it's tough. Running the mine and Themba take up all...*all*...my time.'

'Then it's exceptionally kind of you to take time out for this trip. I'm very grateful.' She settled her hat firmly on her head so it shaded her eyes again. 'But you seem to have a reliable team in place. Are you not happy to leave Themba in their hands while you're away?'

'They're an excellent team, but I prefer to be there. I'm involved in every detail of both operations. I expect to be kept informed about everything and anything, and I don't ask my staff to do anything I wouldn't or couldn't do myself.'

Anna gestured towards the cold box. 'So you've learned to cook?'

She'd intended it to be a light-hearted comment, but Jack simply nodded.

'That's a good example. The restaurant serves world-class meals—sometimes from a surprising collection of ingredients when food deliveries or power supplies have been disrupted. I respect staff who can turn their hands to anything and see adversity as just another challenge. And I know their roles as well as, or better than, they do themselves.'

'Even on the mine?'

'I have an excellent team there, too, headed up by an exceptional manager, but I fly up at least once a fortnight—or immediately if there's a problem. There are not many diamond mines left in private ownership, and it's up to me to see that the highest standards are met all the time.'

'Have you ever considered selling out to one of the big conglomerates? It would make your life a lot easier.'

Jack tossed the half-empty water bottle from one hand to the other, then dropped it into the cold box at their feet.

'There've been offers, but none of them have come with a guarantee to maintain the level of staff welfare and profit-sharing that I've put in place. And, yes, the profit share I take *does* finance Themba, but the diamonds are ethically mined at no human cost. So at the moment selling out is not something I'm considering. An easier life would not necessarily be a better one,' he said slowly. 'As a child I was powerless to prevent some of the bad things that happened at Themba—my mother's death, my father's drinking, the hunting…' He wiped his forehead with the back of one hand. 'I made the decision, a long time ago, never to be powerless again.'

Anna considered the workload he'd taken upon himself and remembered the pallor of exhaustion she'd noticed under his suntan.

'I can understand why your patience would wear thin with trivial requests from annoying guests.'

'Mmm... If you mean Professor Watkins...?' One corner of his mouth lifted in a teasing smile. 'And don't tell me again that you're grown up. I've worked that out.'

Anna ignored the gentle provocation. She wasn't prepared to put her Jack resistance to the test right now. She'd need it all tonight, in that tent on the roof. She glanced up at it and saw him register her look. She thought fast, needing to stamp on that spark of awareness that arced between them, bright and dangerous.

'It must be exhausting, this life you've built for yourself.'

Get back to reality. Extinguish the spark before it becomes a flame.

'Maybe. But this way I have control. The alternative... Well, I've seen that and it's not an option.'

He leaned forward and flipped the lid of the cold box closed. Then he handed her the bottle of water he'd put between them.

'You need to keep hydrated, Anna. I'm sorry— that sounds patronising. I'm sure you remember that this dry heat can be deceptive.'

Anna took the bottle, careful to avoid contact with his fingers. She took a sip.

'What do you mean, Jack? And I don't mean about the heat. I *do* know about that.' She loosened her cotton scarf, marvelling at the fact that it had been cool enough earlier for her to wear her hoodie. 'I mean about the alternative.'

Jack stood up and took two paces away, keeping his back to her. His hands were rammed into his pockets and she saw tension ripple through the muscles across his wide shoulders. His back expanded as he drew in a breath.

'The chaos I inherited is what I mean. My father had lost control of his life—of *everything*. He was mired in a pit of alcohol and guilt and he was powerless to escape the clutches of either of them. It made him furious, and most of that fury was directed at me.'

His voice was so low Anna could barely hear him, but the bitterness in his tone jumped out at her. She sat very still.

'I believe he wanted to die that day. Maybe that's why it happened like it did.'

She allowed a beat of silence to pass before she spoke. 'What happened, Jack?'

Jack turned to face her. Lines of stress etched a frown between his eyes. 'You don't know?'

'I know your father died not long after I left. So what *don't* I know?'

Jack rocked back on his heels.

'I thought everyone knew,' he said, almost to himself. 'It feels as though everyone knows...'

Heat radiated off the surrounding boulders,

sending the temperature to furnace levels. Anna felt its oppressive weight pressing onto her head, into her lungs as she tried to keep her breathing even and quiet.

'Knows what, Jack?'

'That I didn't pull the trigger in time to save him.'

The midday silence was absolute, and then Anna gulped in some air, filling her lungs, giving up the attempt to keep her breathing regular. In her mind's eye she saw again that muscled lion crouching on the track ahead of them. The rifle thrown against Jack's shoulder. She almost felt the imprint of his collarbone on her cheek. Even in the face of extreme, primitive danger she'd felt safe with him.

She stood up and closed the distance between them, holding out a hand. 'Let's get out of the sun.'

They climbed into the vehicle and Jack gunned the engine, but Anna put a hand on his arm.

'It's okay, Anna. We're not going anywhere just yet. I'll just run it for a couple of minutes to cool us down.'

He adjusted the air-conditioning controls and a blast of air hit Anna's face. She turned sideways in her seat.

Jack flipped his head back against the headrest and closed his eyes. They felt gritty with dust and fatigue. He massaged his eye sockets with his knuckles and then crossed his arms again. Someone had once told him it was a defensive gesture, and that was just fine.

'You don't have to tell me—' said Anna.

He interrupted her. 'I do. Because if I don't someone else will.' He stared straight ahead, fixing his gaze on the far horizon. 'My mother died when I was supposed to be looking after her. That was a huge thing for me to deal with—even though I know it was a burden no child should have had to bear. But as if I could make up for it I promised myself that I'd always protect *you*. Keep you safe. You should have been safe with me on Tuesday evening, but the thing is I don't know if you were.' He paused, searching for the right words. 'The hunting business my father ran appalled me. We argued bitterly about it, but I couldn't make him change. After he died I swore no animals would be shot on Themba land ever again unless it was to protect human life or to end a sick or injured animal's suffering if there was no alternative. But I could always see the doubt in the eyes of the trackers. That doubt is the reason Alex tracked the lion we encountered. They just can't be sure of what I'd do. After all, if I didn't shoot to save my father's life, who *would* I save?'

He turned to look at her and found her cool gaze returning his questioning one.

She folded her hands in her lap. 'Please, Jack, start at the beginning and tell me what happened.'

He marvelled at her calmness. Did she suspect he was about to destroy any illusions she still had about him? That he wasn't the man she believed him to be at all. He was conflicted, and confused, and he had to work every minute of every day and frequently a lot of every night to stay sane. Because if he stopped he'd have to confront his demons and answer the question that plagued him.

He hadn't been able to save his mother, and he'd seen his father die because he hadn't squeezed the trigger of his rifle in time. And when he had pulled it, the hopelessly late shot had gone wide anyway. Now, added to all that, he was tormented by the thought that he wouldn't have saved Anna, either.

Sitting here in the midday heat, looking at her, he knew she was the most precious thing in the world to him. His unforgivable lapse in concentration had put her in terrible danger and now he couldn't trust himself to protect her. If anything happened to her he would not be able to live with the unbearable burden of guilt.

Bringing her on this trip, even if it might well turn out to be a disappointing wild goose chase, was the least he could do by way of compensation. If he could help her to put her past to rest he'd have done a good thing. And the next good thing he could do for her would be to put her on that helicopter on Monday morning and wave her goodbye—before he screwed up her life completely.

'Jack?'

'Yeah. Okay.' He gripped the bridge of his nose between his thumb and forefinger and shook his head. 'It was an elephant. The same tusker he'd been hunting for years. Only by then he and the bull were both old, and they were both angry, and one of them was reckless.'

She still didn't look shocked. Those ocean-green eyes hadn't widened. She hadn't gasped... put a hand to her mouth.

'My father went out on his own. When Frank—one of the trackers—suggested going along with him he received a torrent of abuse. Do you remember it was one of the rules...?'

'Never go into the bush alone.' Anna nodded. 'I didn't always comply.'

'No, you didn't.' Jack felt again the jolt of anxiety he associated with her and her alone. 'God, Anna, you kept me in a constant state of high alert, and there were times when I thought I'd lost you...'

'I'm sorry. I should have been more considerate. I think I am now...'

Jack let his eyelids drop and wondered if he'd

ever be able to relax if Anna wasn't in his sights. It felt impossible.

'He'd taken the old Land Rover and Frank and I went after him in the Jeep. Shooting that elephant had become an obsession with him. He'd been hunting him when my mother died, and by some process of twisted logic I think he'd come to blame the elephant for what happened to her.'

'It must have been so difficult for you, Jack…'

Jack remembered with horrible clarity the details of that day. The heat and drought through a long summer had been relentless, and the pale dust which had coated the landscape would only be dispersed by rain. A sense of impending catastrophe had overcome him as he'd raced through the crackling dry bush, trying to reach his father in time.

'I had a good idea of where the old bull was spending most of his days, but by the time we found my father he'd left the vehicle and was staggering towards him, shouting and waving his rifle. He was one of the biggest elephants we've ever had on Themba land. He eyed my father for a few seconds, and I could tell from his elephant body language he wasn't faking it, like they sometimes do. He was about to charge for real. His ears were pinned flat against his head and he'd curled his trunk inwards. He went from nought to full speed in the space of a breath. I'd stopped behind a clump of scrub and got out of the Jeep and I had time to aim. But I was shaking. My usual cool head had deserted me. Watching the disaster unroll felt like a slow-motion movie. It still does.'

'And your father? Did he...?'

Jack shook his head again, frowning. Even after ten years he found it difficult to make sense of what had happened.

'He threw his gun down and stood there with his arms stretched out. Frank yelled at me to shoot. I remember it so clearly. But I didn't. And then my father was gone, under those enormous feet, in a billow of dust. That's when I fired— way too late—and the elephant kept going, right past us. My shot had gone wide. He was so close I could see the expression in his eyes, feel the rush of air whip against my skin.' He put his fingers up to the scar on his forehead. 'A stone flew up from under his feet and cut my face. I only realised later, when blood dripped into my eyes, that I'd been injured. Frank and I ran to my father but he was...gone. His body was crushed and broken, his life snuffed out. It felt...extraordinary. Because seconds earlier he'd been living and breathing. We took him back to Themba and buried him next to my mother, under the baobab tree.'

'Jack...' Anna laid a hand on his shoulder. 'It sounds as if he really was intent on dying. Perhaps he simply couldn't live with his pain any longer. Maybe, somewhere deep down, you knew that you needed to help him let go of it. What good would shooting the elephant have done? It might still have trampled him—and you and Frank, too.'

'Possibly. But the thing is, Frank knew I hadn't acted quickly enough to save him. Now it's what everyone believes. And it's the truth.'

She was quiet for a while, and Jack waited to hear her say she was sure that wasn't the case. That everyone knew he was brave, resolute. Utterly dependable. Instead, her next words were unexpected.

'This may not be the correct thing to say, Jack, but my gut reaction is that I'm *glad* you didn't shoot the elephant. Like I'm glad you didn't shoot the lion.'

She rubbed his shoulder. Jack stared at her, then shook his head.

'I haven't been able to see it that way. I don't think anyone else has, either. I see the questions in their eyes. I see them wondering what sort of man I really am.'

'Has it occurred to you they may simply be concerned for you? They may not be judging you, but you're judging yourself—and harshly. Have you talked about it to anyone? A therapist?'

'Get real, Anna.' His fists gripped the steering wheel. 'Can you see me talking to a therapist?'

His voice dropped as Anna's hand ran down his arm and covered his whitened knuckles. He felt drained and suddenly tired of maintaining this façade of impenetrable strength.

'I haven't had the courage to talk to anybody. Until today.'

'So that's about ten years of internalising the trauma. I don't know how you've kept going, Jack. And you didn't really grieve for your father.'

'Like I said, I could only grieve for the man he might have once been. I felt no sense of loss. All I felt for him was a real, deep anger.'

'That,' said Anna quietly, 'is all part of the process.'

'You sound very sure of your theories.'

'Remember that I lost my parents too, Jack. I have no memories of them, but that doesn't make it easier. In a way it raises even bigger questions. And from what you've told me I'm never going to find any more answers now.'

'I'm sorry if I've destroyed any dreams you had about them. My intention was to help you find some closure, but perhaps this trip was a bad idea. It might make things worse for you.'

'It might, in the short term, but I'm prepared to risk that. I hope it'll help me to draw a line under the past, if nothing else.'

'Is that what you want? To forget the past and move on?'

Regret and sadness wrapped around his heart, but he refused to express those feelings to Anna. Moving on was exactly what he needed her to do.

'Yes, it is.' Her gaze was unwavering. 'And I think that's what you need to do, too.'

Jack didn't know how he could leave his past behind when it had suddenly reappeared, all grown up, back in the centre of his life. Anna was the woman he'd driven himself wild imagining, but his imagination had fallen short of the reality she'd become. Her kind, thoughtful opinion of his actions surrounding his father's death had floored him. He'd been ready to be defensive—aggressive, even—but she'd taken away the need, leaving him unsure how to react.

But he felt strangely better—as if a coiled spring wound tightly inside him had been released and had spent its energy, leaving a calm space where there'd once been turmoil and anger.

All that separated them was the console between the two seats. The heavy gold braid of her hair lay across her shoulder. Jack wanted to lift it out of the way and bury his face in her neck, to breathe in that tantalising perfume. He still hadn't asked what it was. She had bent up one of her endless legs, propping her knee against the gearstick, and he wanted to run his palm up her long thigh and see what his touch would do to her. It would only take a second to reach out and pull her onto his lap…

How would it feel to hold someone in his arms who he cared about? Someone who accepted him for what he was, without reservations or conditions attached? Who wasn't there simply for a luxury weekend at Themba and a couple of nights of great sex.

He realised, with a jolt of regret, that he had absolutely no idea, and wondered why he'd even had the thought. He wasn't in the market for caring. Hell, no. Caring for someone meant you lost them, sooner or later, whether they died or you sent them away.

He wanted to tell Anna how amazing she was, with her compassion and her gentle sympathy, but he couldn't trust himself to frame the words. He'd wanted to kiss her again, on his sofa and then on his deck, but he'd dug deep into his resolve to stop it from happening. That he'd succeeded still surprised him, because he craved the oblivion he knew he'd find if he gave in to those innermost desires. But Anna deserved better than someone using her to forget his guilt for a few moments.

Any affection she showed him now would be the result of pity, and he wouldn't accept that. Sympathy and understanding he could just about deal with. Pity would undo him completely.

He twisted round to straighten up in his seat and fasten his seatbelt. He glanced at his watch. 'We need to get going. At the foot of this hill the track—if we can find it—gets rough, and it'll take us another two hours, at least.'

Out of the corner of his eye he saw Anna nod, and he heard the metallic click as she fastened her own seatbelt. He exhaled a long breath and shoved the gearstick into low gear. Her calm acceptance of his story, the total lack of judgement in her response, had shaken him. He felt as if the wall he'd constructed between himself and the rest of the world had been quietly breached, exposing his vulnerability, threatening his control.

And that scared him more than anything he'd ever encountered in the wild.

CHAPTER SEVEN

MORE THAN TWO bone-shaking hours later, Jack pulled the Land Rover to a stop. Anna eased the death grip she had on the handle above the door and tried to rub some life back into her cramped hands. As the engine shuddered into silence she saw a group of people watching them from the shade of a grove of fever trees.

She glanced across at Jack. 'Are they expecting us?'

'They are.'

Anna raised her eyebrows. 'How come?'

'I sent a message to the mine. I don't know the details of the route it took from there to here, but I knew it would reach the right people. Almost everyone has a phone these days, even if the signal is unreliable. Communications can be dodgy, but something usually works.'

The group consisted of an elderly man who leaned on a tall stick, two middle-aged women, and a young mother with a baby cocooned on her back. As Jack climbed out of the driver's door they moved from the shadows into the sun, towards him.

Jack addressed the man in a dialect Anna didn't recognise. The women studied her with open curiosity, exclaiming to each other and clapping their hands. When Jack spoke to them they nodded, and then one of them gestured towards Anna's face, talking fast.

'They say they remember your eyes, Anna.'

A shiver raised the hairs along Anna's forearms. 'Do you mean these are the people who found me?'

Jack spoke again and they nodded, wide smiles lighting their faces. 'Yes,' he said. 'This man and these two women found you after you'd been flung from the plane as it crashed. This younger woman is the daughter of one of them, and the baby is their granddaughter.'

Emotion and gratitude swelled in Anna's chest as she tried to speak. Had her mother thrown her from the wreckage in a desperate bid to save her before the plane turned into a fireball? Or had her survival simply been luck?

She reached out and squeezed the women's hands in hers as a lump clogged her throat. She looked to Jack for help, and he must have read the plea in her eyes because he spoke again and then translated for her.

'I've told them that you thank them and will be filled with gratitude for their actions for ever.

At least I hope that's what I've said. I'm not fluent in the dialect.'

The elderly man began to walk up the track and beckoned them to follow. Jack fell in beside him, listening as he talked.

'Their village is on that hill.' He pointed. 'He says there was a fierce thunderstorm that afternoon, with a strong wind. The plane came down low, out of the clouds, and then disappeared beyond the trees. There was a loud noise, like more thunder, and flames and thick smoke. Many people ran from the village to help, but the fire was too intense to get close.'

Jack dropped back a pace to walk next to Anna.

'One theory was that they had cans of extra fuel on board. They probably planned to land somewhere remote and refuel. It's why the fire was so intense."

Anna clamped a hand over her mouth to try to hide her distress. She stopped and bent forward, her hands on her knees. 'This is…hard for me to hear.'

He dropped a hand onto her shoulder. 'I'm sorry. Of course it is. Do you want to turn back?'

She straightened up and shook her head. 'No. I must go on. I must see the place.'

Jack nodded once. 'Okay. Just say if it gets too much.'

He strode forward again.

Their progress through the dense bushland was

slow. Vicious thorns snagged at their clothes and insects buzzed in their faces, but eventually they reached the edge of what had evidently once been a clearing. The bushes looked stubby, and the few trees were spindly and half-grown.

Their guide made a sweeping gesture and turned to Jack again.

'He says nothing grew for many years on the burned place, but one day soon all the evidence of a crashed plane will be gone, swallowed up by nature.'

Anna looked around. 'And…me?' Her voice shook. 'Where did they find me?'

The women took her hands and led her to a place on the far side of the space, where young trees grew. They pointed at her, and at the ground, and patted her arms.

Anna stared at the patch of brown dried grass and leaves and wondered how she was supposed to feel. She searched herself for some sort of emotion, however slight. Hearing about the crash and the burning plane had been harrowing, but now all she found in herself was a hollowed-out dark void. She'd imagined this place all her remembered life, and thought about the people who'd carried her to safety. But now that she was here she felt drained and numb.

Nausea churned in her stomach, and she was horribly afraid that she was about to be sick. She wondered why she'd agreed to come. She could have been boarding a flight to Heathrow about now, if she'd chosen the sensible option.

She sensed Jack behind her, felt his hand cup her elbow.

'Do you need a moment on your own?'

She was grateful for his touch, because the warmth of his hand reassured her that she could actually *feel* something. She wanted to lean back and be supported by his broad, solid chest, with his arm gripping her waist to hold her close. If she could tuck her head into his shoulder and feel his cheek on her hair perhaps she'd feel human. Perhaps this would all feel real.

But she lifted her chin and straightened her spine, staying rigidly upright. 'No, thank you. I'll be fine. It just feels weird.' She took a shuddering breath. 'I expected a huge rush of emotion, or some sort of feeling of connection to this place. It's where my parents died, where I only survived by a chance twist of fate, but I don't feel anything apart from sick.'

She turned to look at him, to see if he understood.

'I can't sense anything of them here. Anything at all.'

They made their way back to the Land Rover, the silence broken only by their feet swishing through the grass and the young mother crooning a song to her baby.

Anna folded her arms across her stomach and

turned to Jack. 'Please will you thank them again? I'm very grateful.' She lifted her shoulders. 'What can I possibly say to the people who literally saved my life?'

Jack nodded and translated her words, and they all raised their hands in farewell. The villagers turned away and Jack opened the car door for her. She stared straight ahead as he started the engine and turned the vehicle.

'I'm sorry, Anna.' Jack twisted his head to look at her. 'I underestimated how traumatic this would be for you. I think it was a bad idea.'

She shook her head. 'No. It was the right thing to do.' She pushed the seatbelt buckle into its slot with more force than necessary. 'I'll always be grateful to you for bringing me here, but I won't need to come again. And I don't want the diamonds, but I don't know what to do with them.'

Jack found a place for their overnight camp on a bluff overlooking an almost dry riverbed, where the view to the west stretched on for ever. He made a fire and boiled water for tea, then pulled a can of beer from the cold box.

He watched Anna, where she sat with her legs dangling out of the passenger side of the vehicle. Her gaze appeared to be fixed on the horizon, but he suspected it was really turned inwards, doing some soul-searching.

Since leaving the village she hadn't uttered a

word. Her silence didn't surprise him. It had been a stressful, emotional day, and he thought she was probably suffering from the slump that often followed an adrenaline overload.

He handed her a mug of tea and propped himself against the side of the vehicle, rolling the can of beer between his palms. 'Want to talk?'

'Not about this afternoon.' She took the mug of tea and sipped. 'The sunset is spectacular.'

'Mmm... Possibly too spectacular.' He flipped up the ring-pull on the can and peeled it back. The beer hissed and foamed. 'Those storm clouds are some distance away, but they look as if they mean business.'

Mountainous thunderheads were heaped on the western horizon. Arrows of red and pink, fired by the sinking sun, radiated from behind the bright gold which traced their edges.

'Do you think it'll rain? Tonight?' she asked.

Jack lifted a shoulder. 'Maybe. But I hope we'll make it back to Themba before there's a deluge.' He tipped back his head and took several swallows of beer. 'We want the rain, but not while we're out here.' He drummed his fingers against the can. 'You know how ferocious early summer storms can be. We should get an early night and be away at first light. After we've eaten I'll sort out the tent, and you can get settled while I clear up down here.'

'Okay.' She peered over her shoulder into the

back of the vehicle. 'But are you sure it wouldn't be…better if I slept in there?'

Jack emptied the rest of the beer down his throat and crumpled the can in his fist. The hell she'd sleep in the boot. Wherever she slept, it was going to be with him, so that he knew she wasn't wandering off in the night to paddle in what was left of the river with the hippos and the crocs. He wanted her where he could feel her breathing next to him…where he could reach out and put his arm around her waist to keep her there if he had to.

He knew he had to stop treating her like a child and start accepting her as the responsible adult she'd become, but he told himself she'd been traumatised. She needed watching. He could keep her safe for these last few days.

And if that felt like an excuse he could live with it.

At some point that icy composure was going to shatter, and he needed to be there to keep the pieces of Anna together when it happened. That was all, he told himself. There was no other reason. He'd proved he could resist her, after all.

He hoped the shake of his head as he answered was convincingly dismissive.

'No. I can see you're worn out. Today has been long and emotional, and the drive wasn't easy, either. Besides…' he threw her a half-smile '…I need you where I can keep an eye on you.

You don't have the best record for staying where you're meant to be.'

He thought she'd laugh, or at least smile and acknowledge that he was right, but she just shrugged, shaking out the dregs of tea from the mug.

'Okay.'

They sat on folding canvas stools, and he was pleased to see her eat one of the hot dogs he assembled. He hoped the glass of red wine she'd swallowed in three gulps would relax her enough for sleep.

When she shivered he unrolled a blanket and dropped it over her shoulders. 'I'll build up the fire. You'll sleep better if you go to bed warm.'

'Thanks.'

'I can make you some hot chocolate, if you like.'

She shook her head. 'I'm fine.'

He knew she was far from fine. It felt as if the air between them crackled with unspoken words and half-formed thoughts. But he also knew better than to probe. He remembered how he'd felt in the aftermath of his father's violent death. How it had taken him years to process it and he still had not come to terms with it. The death of Anna's parents had also been horrifying, and she was still only just beginning the process of grieving all these years later.

He picked up the bottle of wine and held it out to her, then topped up his own glass when she declined.

She stood up and bundled the blanket into the boot. 'I'll…go to bed. If that's okay.'

She'd managed the whole evening without once looking directly at him.

'Sure,' he said easily. 'I'll see you in the morning. If we make an early start we'll beat the storm, if it's coming our way. You'll be able to sleep in your own bed tomorrow night.'

'My own bed,' she said over her shoulder, 'is a long way from Themba.'

He heard her sluice water from the big plastic bottle over her face and neck, and brush her teeth, and then she climbed up the ladder and disappeared into the tent. The battery lantern he'd left burning cast her flickering shadow against the canvas sides. When the movements stopped he assumed she'd settled down to sleep.

He took his time packing up, then added more wood to the fire and watched it burn down while he tuned in to the night sounds. When he'd suggested identifying what they could hear earlier Anna had said she was too tired. The temperature had fallen sharply with the fading light, and now a sneaky breeze curled up from the riverbed, raising a shiver along his arms. Finally, when he'd run out of reasons not to, he closed the tailgate as softly as possible, kicked over the embers of the fire and climbed up into the tent.

Anna slept curled up in her sleeping bag, her knees wedged against the side of the tent. She'd pulled the hood of her top up over her head. Jack moved carefully, stowing his boots next to hers near the zipped-up entrance and sliding, fully clothed, into his own sleeping bag. He stretched out, flicked off the lantern and tucked a folded arm behind his head.

He stared into the darkness, listening to the measured rise and fall of Anna's breathing, and ran the events of the day through his head once more. He'd never verbalised how he'd watched his father die to anyone, and while he recognised that talking had been cathartic, it had drained him emotionally. He felt raw and exposed. And on top of that he'd watched Anna go through all kinds of hell this afternoon, although she'd insisted she was fine. She might feel nothing now, but that protective numbness would wear off and then her emotional reaction might be unexpected in its ferocity.

He wished she'd confide in him...spill the thoughts he was sure were churning behind those opaque evergreen eyes. He wished he could close the small space between them and spoon her so that when she woke she wouldn't feel so alone.

He wasn't expecting to fall asleep any time

soon. It might have been a long day, but it was going to be a very long night.

Jack went from sleep to full-on alert in the time it took him to open his eyes in the absolute darkness of the tent. He lay motionless, every muscle tensed, every nerve-ending tuned in to the silence.

Something was wrong, and that something was the silence.

He knew without stretching out his arm to find her, without straining to hear her quiet breathing, that he was alone.

Anna had gone.

He swore and pushed himself upright, struggling to kick his way out of the sleeping bag and find the lantern at the same time. How had she done this? Only inches separated them. The zip of the tent's entrance was not quiet. When had he ever slept through even the slightest disturbance?

He swore again as his groping hand knocked the lantern over and it rolled out of reach. He cursed himself for not having his powerful torch in bed with him. What use was it stowed in the vehicle? His fingers, clumsy with shock and hurry, fumbled for the zipper. Finally locating the metal tab, he tugged at it, ripping it upwards and pushing the flaps aside.

His hands made contact with something soft, blocking his way out.

'Jack?'

Her voice, even though it was barely a whisper in the dark, felt like a punch in the chest, relieving his lungs of oxygen. The air rasped in his throat as he dragged it back.

'*Anna?* I thought...' His searching hands found her shoulders, the long braid of her hair, the curve of her neck. 'I thought you'd gone.' His heart slammed against his ribs and his breath was quick. 'What the hell are you *doing*?'

Her narrow shoulders, swamped by the hoodie, shifted under his hands. 'I woke up. I needed some air. Some space.'

Jack closed his eyes and sent a prayer of thanks to whoever might be listening out here in the wild. The vivid scenario which had flashed through his mind fully formed, of having to try to find her before something bigger and hungrier beat him to it, faded. He tried to control the tremor which seized him, and he closed his hands around her upper arms.

'You scared me stupid, Anna. It's... Are you okay?'

A translucent slice of moon hung low in the sky, no competition for the light from the stars. They glimmered like splinters of crystal flung by some giant hand across black velvet. He felt that lift of her shoulders again and she angled her head towards him.

'I feel...lost.'

He caught the gleam of dampness on her cheek

'I don't want to know anything more about my past. It doesn't sound good. And the future I thought I wanted seems...out of reach.'

'Hey...' Jack bent his knees and put his arms around her ribcage, shuffling her backwards until she leant against him. He tried to ignore the perfect fit of her thighs between his, the snug contact with his groin. 'Yesterday was all a bit of an overload. Things will feel more manageable in daylight. They always do.'

He thought he felt her body grow a fraction heavier as she relaxed. Her breathing settled, her ribs expanding and then flattening against his abdomen.

'Look up, Anna. The stars are incredible.' He needed the distraction as much as she did.

'Mmm... They are. I'd forgotten how bright they are out here. No light pollution.'

'None at all.'

'It's like being inside an upside-down bowl of stars. They shine all the way down to the horizon.'

Jack raised a hand, smoothing her hair back from her forehead and settling her head into his shoulder. This was Anna, he reminded himself, and he needed to look after her and make her feel better.

'Do you remember the story of how the Milky Way was formed?' he asked.

He felt her head move as she searched for the

dense pathway of millions of stars which wove its way across the night sky.

'There was a girl who wanted to provide light so that her people could find their way home...' Anna wriggled her shoulders, settling further into the crook of his arm. 'She flung the ashes from her mother's fire into the air and the ashes became the stars of the Milky Way.'

Jack nodded, his cheek rubbing against her hair. 'That was one of the first stories I told you. When the sun rises tomorrow you'll feel different. You'll know what you want.'

'I've always known what I want, Jack.'

He thought he knew what she wanted: a proper home and family, to make up for never having had one of her own. A real bricks and mortar house, not a collection of thatched huts. A husband. And two point four children.

During her school holidays she used to return to Themba and describe to him the details of her visits to schoolfriends' homes. She'd been intrigued by the workings and dynamics of those 'normal' families.

He could give her his protection, but he could never give her that kind of stifling security. He'd seen the havoc a reckless, selfish man could wreak on his family, and he was never, ever going to risk seeing history repeat itself through him. He'd vowed years ago to stay away from commitment, family and anything resembling...*love*.

He had trouble forcing himself even to form the word as a thought.

His mother must have loved his father to put up with the years of hardship and neglect she'd suffered, and look what had happened to her. He could never risk putting any woman through that. The only love he'd witnessed had been destructive, and it had ultimately led to loss. It wasn't something he was willing to experience ever again.

He shifted a little, remembering the way he'd shattered Anna's dreams eleven years ago. He'd laid the blame for sending her away at the feet of those men, circling her like hyenas closing in on a defenceless gazelle. But he hadn't been able to trust himself, either—although it had taken him a long time to admit that. He'd had to get her away. He'd meant it when he'd said he never wanted a wife. That didn't mean he hadn't wanted *her*.

Now he wanted her grown-up self even more, and that made the situation they were in perilous.

Her seductive perfume invaded his senses, playing havoc with his responses, and her hair slid like silk against his sensitised skin. Beneath the bulky hoodie the curves which had developed from her teenager's skinny frame filled his arms perfectly. He tried to ease himself away from her, alarmed at the sudden urgency of the sensations building in his body. He'd resisted them before. He could do it again.

He sucked the cool night air into his lungs and raised his head. 'Can I get you something that'll help you sleep, Anna? Is there anything you need?'

Her head fell back revealing the sweep of her cheek, her full lower lip, the starlight reflected in her eyes.

'What I really need, Jack, is for you to kiss me.'

Jack felt as if the universe had paused along with his breathing. He could do the sensible thing—put space between them and tell her he didn't want to kiss her. Or he could abandon sense completely and do what they both wanted, what they desperately needed, more than anything else.

Inches separated their lips. Her eyes were just a gleam in the dark, her face a pale oval. He raised one hand and cupped her cheek in his palm, running an unsteady thumb across her cheekbone.

'Anna…'

'Please, Jack.'

He dropped his head a fraction and rested his forehead against hers.

'Anna, I don't know…'

Her hand drifted up and cupped the back of his head, her fingers tunnelling into his hair.

'Jack, I know we shouldn't. I know you're trying to be sensible. But I just…need you. Now.'

She lifted her head and he felt the feather-light

brush of her lips along his jaw, pausing at the corner of his mouth.

Jack sighed out a breath and his lips found hers. They tasted of sweet peppermint, and he could swear a hint of that peach she'd eaten earlier still lingered on them, but perhaps he was confusing it with her scent.

He fought to keep the kiss gentle and light, barely touching her. There would still be a way back from that. But she reached for more, pulling his head down and sealing their lips together.

Her soft sweetness melted under his mouth as molten desire poured through his body, unstoppable as hot lava. He heard her moan in her throat as he deepened the kiss and he thought it was a muttered 'yes'. His tongue traced the join of her lips, parting them with its tip, allowing himself to go further, to invade her warm mouth.

They'd shared one hot kiss, but this was becoming off-the-scale scorching. He probed deep, his tongue tangling with hers, then withdrew to take her bottom lip in his mouth to suck on it. Anna gasped, responding with thrusts of her own tongue. She twisted towards him, flattening her body against his, as if she needed to obliterate any gaps that remained between them.

Jack hauled her across his lap. Her arms wrapped around his neck, clamping him against her body so he could feel the push of her breasts against his chest. He rested a hand on her waist, then found the edge of the ridiculously big hoodie and the hem of her tee shirt. He felt her stomach muscles contract, making space for his hand to move under her clothes, and then heard the sharp intake of her breath as his exploring fingers found her smooth, hot skin. Her breathing turned quick and shallow as he moved his hand upwards, finally cupping the silk-covered mound of her breast before his thumb drifted across the puckered nipple.

'Oh, Jack...'

'Do you want me to stop, Anna? If you do...'

Her answer was to pick up his hand in hers. He didn't know where he'd find the self-control, but if that was what she wanted, he would listen. But she guided his hand down, to the inside of her thigh. Her legs shifted and he realised what she wanted. His fingers stroked upwards, increasing their pressure until he felt her damp heat through the cotton of her clothes. She lifted her hips towards him and cried out against his mouth as her whole body tensed. Then she relaxed, limp in his arms.

Jack gathered her against him as she shuddered twice. He listened as her rapid breathing slowed into a deeper rhythm and felt her heartbeat begin to steady. Frustration welled up in him but he fought it, denying his own need. Anna was relaxed at last. She seemed to be deeply asleep.

He dropped a kiss on her cheek. To hold her was enough.

He inched back into the tent, pulling her with him, then slid her from his arms onto the mattress, putting a pillow under her head. She sighed and turned onto her side, drawing her knees up. Jack unzipped his sleeping bag and unfolded it. Then he lay down next to her, spreading it over them and putting an arm across her waist. He closed his hand around her slender fingers and tucked her head under his chin.

She wouldn't be able to move an inch without him knowing about it.

Anna woke slowly, dragging herself out of a deep, dreamless sleep, and it took her a few moments to work out where she was. Heavy lethargy weighted her body. And then she realised something had pinned her down. She raised her eyelids and saw that it was an arm, clad in a checked cotton shirt, and that the hand belonging to it had her own hand loosely clasped in long, strong fingers.

Jack. Her brain engaged with reluctance, and then the memories of the night began to unroll. He must have put her back to bed after... Her cheeks heated as she remembered what they'd done...what *she'd* done. But even as embarrassment made her want to squirm, pleasure at the memory, intense and undeniable, spiked through her, kicking up the beat of her heart and sending arrows of renewed desire deep into her body.

His breathing altered a fraction and she knew he'd woken.

'Anna?'

'Mmm…?'

He shifted behind her, inching away, but not before she felt the hard imprint of him against the small of her back.

She felt him move, propping himself on one elbow. She turned her head. His dark hair, tousled from sleep, flopped over his forehead and rough stubble shadowed his jaw. Eyes, iron-grey and serious, regarded her. Need pierced her and she wanted to turn into his arms and lose herself again under the sweet magic of his skilled mouth, the stroke of his tongue and the caress of his clever fingers.

But sex with Jack was not part of her plan. Her plan was to be cool and professional. To prove to him that she could come back to Africa, to Themba…okay, to *him*…and handle it all with the control worthy of an ice queen. And then she'd turn her back and return to her life. The real, proper life that she'd begun to build for herself with painful care. Which was what she wanted— what she told herself she'd always wanted.

Last night had been a blip…the consequence of a traumatic, tiring and in the end shattering, day. She'd needed something, someone, to hijack her thoughts…to stop the endless churning of *if onlys* and *what ifs* in her head. It had been Jack who'd delivered her to sweet oblivion. But it could have been anyone. Couldn't it?

She caught her lip between her teeth and dragged her eyes away from the face that constantly got in the way of her determination to live life on her own terms. She looked beyond him, over his shoulder, to distract herself.

'Are you okay?' His voice was gravelly, sexy as sin.

'Are you?' she asked.

'Frustrated as all hell and short of sleep.'

Anna blinked, surprised by his candour. 'I'm… sorry, Jack.' She turned onto her back. 'I shouldn't have done that. I just needed to…to forget for a while. Perhaps it's selfish, but I don't think we should continue…'

There was a beat of silence and then Jack rolled over and sat up, his back to her. The tension across his wide shoulders screamed for her to stretch out her hands and massage those muscles until they relaxed.

'Of course we shouldn't. So let's forget it.' He pushed a hand through his hair. 'Anyway, it's late. We need to go.'

CHAPTER EIGHT

DESPITE THE BLAST of cold air from the air-conditioning unit, the atmosphere inside the vehicle felt as sultry and threatening as the day outside. They'd packed up in near-silence and Anna had refused any breakfast. Contrary to Jack's promise of the night before, nothing looked better in the morning. For starters, the sun hadn't come out. Also she was confused, and sad, and she wanted him with an ache that shocked her. No amount of silent, sensible reasoning would soothe that.

A leaden sky hung above them. The air felt sluggish and thick, and the land seemed to crouch, sullen, beneath its weight, holding its breath. Jack looked to the west as he swung himself into the driver's seat.

'It's already raining in the mountains. We don't have much time.'

Anna wanted to ask how much time they didn't have. And what would happen when it ran out. But Jack's set jaw and the lines around his straight mouth, the frown of concentration between his brows, stopped her. She'd find out soon enough, and right now she had to concentrate on holding on to the handle above the door as Jack depressed the accelerator and the Land Rover lurched over rocks and the mounds of ant hills.

When they reached the track he put on more speed, and she felt relieved that talking had become impossible.

Did he resent what had happened last night? Had he expected her to take it further this morning? To ask him to make love to her? Or for her to take control and make love to him? She'd wanted to. God, how much she'd wanted to. But that wasn't how things were going to be between them.

She had her own path to follow and it led her away from Themba. He had his, too, and she knew it was nowhere near wide enough for her to be at his side. Once she would have been grateful to follow behind him, hoping he'd occasionally turn around and include her in some aspect of his life. That was no longer an option.

She kept her head turned away and stared out of the window at the bush racing past. She thought about the email which had dropped into her inbox two days ago. It contained a permanent job offer from the zoo in San Diego, to head up their big cat conservation project. It was everything she'd ever wanted since that long-ago day when she'd accepted there'd never be a place for her at Themba, with Jack.

She wondered why she hadn't accepted it immediately.

She thought of Brett, a sexy doctor of marine biology, and the message he'd pinged to her phone earlier in the week.

I miss my beach buddy. When are you coming back?

Brett spent his working life under the ocean and most of his leisure time on its surface, surfing or swimming. His laid-back Californian approach to life was sharply at odds with her driven determination.

'Come to the beach with me,' he'd say, appearing at her desk in board shorts and flip-flops, and she'd be charmed away from her research by his slow smile and warm brown eyes.

She knew beach buddies could easily become bed buddies. And then what?

She frowned, because her imagination always stalled on that thought.

Her attention bounced back to the present as the vehicle slewed to a stop and Jack pushed open his door.

'Hear that?'

For a moment Anna thought a part of her mind had remained in Southern California. The distant rumble sounded like the big rollers of the Pacific, powering ashore. But as it echoed off the rocky cliffs on the far side of the riverbed they were following she nodded, fully present.

'That's the storm breaking. We need to get out of the valley. There'll be a flash flood, for sure.'

He slammed the door and gravel spat from under the wheels as the vehicle accelerated.

A twinge of anxiety snagged at Anna and she twisted to look at him.

'What time will we get back?' She had to shout above the roar of the engine.

'Mid-afternoon...' His attention was fixed on the winding track. 'If we can keep going at this pace.'

He swerved around a boulder and Anna was flung sideways, her shoulder hitting the door.

'We should have left at first light. I could smell the rain coming last night.'

She slapped away a twinge of guilt. It was her fault they'd overslept, but if they'd made love this morning, as she knew he'd wanted to, they'd have been even later.

The track climbed up out of the valley to higher ground and Anna felt her tension ease. They'd be safe from a flash flood now. She counted the hours to when she could sink into a steaming hot bath in her suite and allow all the sadness and confusion of the past two days to dissolve. She'd think about the job offer. Ask for more details.

Mentally, she began to compose a reply to Brett.

Hunger gnawed at her, and she wished she'd had breakfast after all, but Jack's grim expression and reluctance to talk had tied her stomach into a tight knot. Now she decided to try to re-establish something of the rapport they'd tentatively begun to build.

'Can we stop for something to eat?'

He threw a glance at her and then returned his eyes to the road.

'We need to keep going.'

'But we're out of the valley. We're safe from the flood—if it even happens.'

She kept her eyes away from his fingers as he gripped the gearstick and changed down to power up a steep incline.

'It'll happen. And we're on the wrong side of the river, Anna. Remember the ford yesterday morning? We need to get back across that before it's submerged.'

Anna remembered the low concrete causeway. It had no railings at the sides and crouched low over the riverbed. A few muddy puddles dotted the area around it. An eight-foot Nile crocodile had been sunning itself on a sandbank.

'But the river was almost dry, Jack, and it's not raining.'

'It's been raining in the west since the early hours of the morning. That thunder is the storm getting going. The flood will be on its way. We just have to beat it to the causeway.' He swore under his breath. 'It's my fault. I was awake until dawn and then I overslept.'

'That was my fault,' Anna said, staring straight ahead.

Jack removed a hand from the steering wheel and furrowed his fingers through his hair. 'No. It's my responsibility to keep us...*you*...safe.'

A jagged fork of white lightning split the purple sky, followed a second later by the crack of thunder. A sudden splatter of fat raindrops hit the windscreen, joining up to create rivulets of mud on the dust-caked glass.

'Damn.' Jack slammed the heel of one hand against the steering wheel. 'We're not going to make it.' He braked hard and the big four-by-four skidded to a halt. 'Come and look.'

Anna slid out of her seat and joined Jack where he stood on the shoulder of the dirt road.

'Watch the bend in the river.'

As she fixed her eyes on the spot he'd indicated Anna became aware of a distant dull roar, separate from the thunder. The noise built with every second and it triggered a memory.

She'd been standing on top of the rocky outcrop behind Themba, her arms stretched wide, her head tipped back. A storm had been raging around her, the wind whipping her hair into a tangle and rain bouncing off the rocks. Then a figure had burst from the huts below. It had been

Jack, shouting at her to come down, that it was dangerous to be on the rocks during a storm because the ironstone attracted lightning strikes.

She'd been mesmerised by the spectacle nature was staging for her, and Jack had had to climb the boulders and drag her, protesting, to safety. But she'd seen the wall of water, several feet high, roaring through the valley, engulfing the low bridge and spreading a brown, choppy blanket out across the dry bush. Back under cover, Jack had shouted at her, white-faced and shaking, about disappearing on her own and getting hurt.

She'd glared at him, puzzled. 'But I'm not hurt. And *you're* not the boss of me.' She'd stamped a foot.

'I am,' Jack had said, his chest heaving. 'Because if I'm not, who is?'

'Nobody! I'm the boss of myself!'

She'd stomped off to her hut.

Now Anna watched a repeat of that flood on a much bigger scale. The wall of water thundering around the bend in the river was higher, wider and moving much more quickly. It lapped against the foot of the cliffs below the place where they stood, and on the far side it spread inexorably outwards, dislodging rocks, uprooting bushes and shunting logs in front of it. The wave roared past them, leaving an expanse of muddy water churning in its wake.

Jack turned to her. 'I'm sorry.'

'Sorry?' She shrugged. 'It's not your fault, Jack. I know you control everything at Themba, but not even you can control the weather.'

'No, but I can... I *should* be able to control my own behaviour. Things went wrong last night and I overslept this morning. It was a misjudgement, and now I've put you in danger.'

Anna stared at him. 'I think, Jack, that it was *I* who should have had more control last night. But you know what? I'm *not* sorry. I'm also *not* your responsibility. Not any more. You have to change your thinking.'

Jack shook his head, his eyes fixed on hers. 'I can't. I've tried, and I can't. I promised I'd always look after you. What if something happened to you? I'd...'

Another flash of white light ripped through the inky sky and thunder crackled sharply overhead. In a few seconds the rain changed from single heavy drops exploding in the dust at their feet into saturating sheets of what felt like solid water.

Jack threw an arm across Anna's shoulders and bent to shout in her ear. 'Get under cover!'

He hustled her to the passenger door and she scrambled in, but she was already wet. She swiped water out of her eyes as he leapt into the driver's seat.

'What now, Jack? Do we sit it out here? For how long?'

He shook his head, flicking his hair off his

forehead. 'We must keep going, before the roads are all knee-deep in mud. I'll see if I can get Themba on the radio. We might be within range.'

'Are we on Themba land?'

'Yeah. Just. And there's one option…'

He picked up the radio handset and flicked switches. Static crackled and then she heard a voice.

Deafened by successive claps of thunder, Anna couldn't make a lot of sense of Jack's half of the conversation, but when he'd finished he turned to her. His eyes held relief, but she could sense apprehension in him, too.

'If we can make it to the treehouse we'll be okay.'

'The *treehouse*?'

The shaky platform they'd visited as children, miles from the main camp, hardly merited the title. It had consisted of a few planks, barely held together by old rope, wedged in the canopy of a massive ebony tree which grew on the edge of a deep ravine. Jack's father had used it as a game-spotting platform.

'Would that be the same treehouse…?'

'Yeah. But it's undergone a renovation. A couple in the party arriving tomorrow have booked it for two nights, so it's all stocked and ready.'

'But we can't use it, Jack, if your guests need it.'

Jack revved the engine and inched the wheels

back onto the slick surface of the road, switching the wipers to their fastest speed. He raised his voice so he could be heard above the drumming of the downpour on the roof.

'They're coming by road from another reserve. They won't make it tomorrow. It's going to be days before anyone can get in or out of Themba.'

'My flight...'

'No chance.'

'But what about the helicopter? Why can't...?'

'The helicopters will be busy lifting food and medical supplies to communities cut off by the floods. Perhaps you've been away too long to remember this is Africa, Anna. The land of wild and fierce extremes, where nothing is predictable.'

Mud churned beneath the wheels and twice the vehicle lurched dangerously towards the edge of the track. More than once Jack had to stop, reverse, and try a different way.

The storm raged without let-up, ear-splitting and ferocious, pouring torrents of rain from the swollen clouds.

When it seemed at its most intense Jack swung the wheel and took a smaller track which had become little more than a gushing stream. The water rushed past them at wheel-arch-height and Anna expected it to seep through the doors and swamp her feet at any moment. Then they stopped. Jack cut the engine and peered through the windscreen.

'It's not far from here. We'll have to run. Just don't let go of my hand.'

Anna was soaked to the skin as soon as she left the shelter of the vehicle. Water swirled around her legs. She tugged her hood over her head and gripped Jack's hand. Then they ran, splashing through the water, slipping on the mud. She stumbled, but Jack yanked her to her feet and kept going uphill, through the hammering rain. She was half dragged up a flight of wooden steps, and then Jack paused and pulled keys from a box beside a solid wooden door. He pushed her ahead of him, out of the rain.

The door slammed, shutting out the storm. Above them the thatch muffled the sound of the rain and the thunder seemed more distant. Their breathing sounded loud and ragged in the relative quiet. Anna's shoulders heaved and her lungs burned while her racing heart tried to play catch-up. She glanced around, and in the gloom could make out the massive tree trunk which rose through the centre of the space. A polished wooden floor stretched around it, and folding glass doors, sealed against the weather, let in pale light, filtered through the leaves.

Jack stood in front of her, pushing his dripping hair off his forehead, water pooling at his feet.

His plaid shirt was plastered across his broad chest and his rain-darkened cargo pants clung to his braced thighs. His eyes, grey as the spring storm outside, were lit with silver flames.

He took a step towards her. 'Welcome to Ebony Tree Lodge.'

'Thank you.'

She felt suddenly awkward. A rivulet of water trickled its way down her plait and discharged itself in a tiny cascade to the floor. Jack raised a hand and took hold of the end of her pigtail and squeezed some of the water out of it. Their eyes locked. The magnetism of the connection between them felt too powerful for Anna to break. She swayed on her feet and saw concern flicker across his face. He moved closer, sliding his hand from her hair to her shoulder.

'Jack...?' Her voice sounded distant. 'I...'

He was so close she could feel the warmth from his body, but she shivered.

'You're cold, Anna. We need to get you warm.' His voice was soft, almost a murmur, as he eased the hood away from her face and pushed it back.

'Not cold. But...' Her breath shallowed and she pressed a hand to her chest to try and still her heartbeat. Jack's fingers drifted across her jaw and dropped to the place at her throat where she knew her pulse was thudding out of control. As he watched her his clean scent swirled through her senses, making her feel dizzy, and his eyes became her one fixed point of reference.

She heard the rain on the thatch, the wind lashing the branches of the tree above and around them, and she felt utterly safe, cocooned in this space with him, disconnected from everything in the world except each other.

She put a palm against Jack's chest and felt his powerful heartbeat through the wet cotton, his pecs solid under the fabric. Her hand flattened against the hard bead of a nipple.

His breath stuttered in his chest and he raised his head. 'Anna. Are you sure?'

She nodded, not trusting her voice. Sex with Jack was not what she'd planned, but it was what she'd wanted for what felt like for ever, with every clamouring cell in her body. She could still be cool. Still walk away afterwards, back to the life she was meant to lead, she told herself. What could be more grown-up than that?

His hands closed around her upper arms and he pulled her towards him, wrapping her tightly and burying his face in her damp hair. Then he tipped her head back and rested his forehead against hers.

'You'll never know how much I've wanted you,' he muttered against her mouth. 'You've invaded my very soul.'

And as their lips met it felt to Anna as if they

were in the eye of their own private storm as it
broke around them inside the treehouse.

Jack interrupted the intensely erotic kiss only
long enough to pull the wet hoodie up and over
her head. He tossed it aside and then his fingers
tangled with the buttons of the shirt she'd put on
this morning, in place of the *Save the Whales*
tee shirt. Impatience seethed through him and he
gripped the edges and ripped them apart, sending
pearly shell buttons skittering across the floor.
His big hands circled her ribcage, then he moved
them up to cup her breasts, feathering his thumbs
over their iron-hard peaks.

'Anna.' He kissed her hard. 'I want to look at
you, but I can't wait.'

He squatted and pulled off her boots, and his
own, then reached up and helped her with the
zipper of her cargo pants. He hooked his fingers
into the waistband and began to ease them over
her hips with her briefs, tugging at the saturated
fabric where it stuck to her wet skin and then lifting first one of her feet and then the other away.
He straightened up, holding her pelvis steady and
running his mouth from the vee where her thighs
joined up over her tummy to the groove between
her breasts.

He felt her fingers tug at the buckle of his belt.
Somehow he helped her to drag his wet clothes
off, and then he walked her backwards until her

spine rested against the tree trunk. As he lifted her she coiled her legs around him and rocked her hips. He gasped, trying to slow down.

She was experienced, he could tell, and wild with the need which had simmered between them for years. Jealousy arced through him at the thought of any other man touching her, making love to her.

Get a grip, Eliot. Did you expect her to save herself for you?

He took several deep breaths, trying to hold her still. 'Anna, wait...'

Supporting her, although it was clear she didn't want to wait, he carried her through the open-plan living area, shouldered a screen aside and pulled back the mosquito netting which hung around a wide bed. Then he eased himself down onto the white linen cover, taking her with him. She clung to his shoulders and protested when he tried to move away, so he stretched out one hand to find what he needed in the bedside cabinet.

His fingers located the foil packet and he breathed a quick sigh of relief. The treehouse was, indeed, equipped down to the last detail.

As he slid into her warm, ready body she arched her back and he drew a rosy nipple into his mouth. The silk which covered it created an unbearably erotic friction between his tongue and her skin. He heard her cry out, and then he was flying, carrying her with him in his arms.

He cradled the back of Anna's head in one hand and buried his face against her shoulder. She sighed on an unsteady breath and he raised his head to look at her. Long lashes lay against her flushed cheeks. Her heart thundered against his ribs. When he shifted his position a little her thighs tightened around his hips.

He reached down and grabbed the soft throw which lay folded at the foot of the bed and pulled it over them. Her body, lying under his, felt utterly relaxed. His fingers stroked tendrils of her hair off her forehead, making space for him to place his lips on her dewy skin. Then he couldn't stop himself from brushing a thumb across her cheek. He wanted to keep her here, like this, for ever.

She opened her eyes. 'That was…'

'It was.'

'Can we do it again?'

She pulled a hand from under the blanket and folded it in his. He felt the tightening begin in his groin again.

'Since this is the only bed, and we're stuck in this tree, I think the answer to that is definitely a yes. But first I'm going to run a bath for you. Or for us, if you prefer. And then…'

'A bath? In a treehouse?'

'No luxury has been spared.' He wound his fingers through a strand of her hair. 'And then we'll eat whatever delicious food has been left for the poor guests who are missing out on this incredible experience.'

'Should I feel guilty?'

'Not on their behalf. They can come later in the week—if they can get here. And if you feel guilty about anything else…?'

'Nothing.'

He studied her face, believing she was being honest. So there was nobody else in her life at the moment, then.

Shut those thoughts down, Eliot. Anyone else in her life is nothing to do with you. Nothing at all.

Should he hope there was someone else? So there was no chance of her wanting to stay, asking him for what he couldn't give? He wouldn't think about it. He had her here—they had each other here—for two days, max, while the floodwaters drained away. Then they'd return to Themba, and she to London and California, to the proper life she wanted.

He shifted a little and her eyelids fluttered to her cheeks again. He eased himself away from her and bent his head to kiss her mouth.

'Don't go, Jack.'

'I'll come back…and then I'll carry you to the bathroom. The view from the bath is stunning, but it's too dark to see now. We'll have to have another bath tomorrow.'

He padded from the room and found matches in the kitchen area, so he could light the oil lamps.

The solar power had done its work during the day and the bathwater was hot. He tipped a generous slug of lemon-scented bath oil into it. White linen bathrobes hung on hooks. He slung a towel around his hips, carried a robe to the bedroom and lit more lamps...warm globes of light blossoming in the dusk.

'It's still raining heavily, but I think we'll find everything we need here. Tomorrow I can get anything you want from the Land Rover.' He held up the robe. 'Until your clothes are dry you can wear this.'

Anna had propped a mound of pillows behind her and pulled the throw up around her shoulders. She'd undone her hair and it shone like dark gold brocade across the white linen. She stretched out a hand and circled his wrist, tugging at it until he sat down on the edge of the bed. The cashmere throw clung to the curves of her body beneath it...curves which he wanted to explore, slowly and in great detail, with his hands and his mouth.

'I don't think my shirt is fit for purpose any more—wet or dry. And although this treehouse is equipped down to the last detail, I don't think that includes a kit for sewing on buttons.'

Anna shrugged and the throw slipped a little. A dimple showed in her cheek.

'Contraceptives but no sewing kit. Who dictated those priorities?'

'I'll let you guess.'

Her skin glowed creamy in the lamplight and he couldn't drag his eyes away from the exposed curve of her breast, covered in lacy silk, still damp from his mouth.

'I might decide to go topless. I'm guessing nobody can see in.'

'Then we won't be leaving the bed, so having no clothes won't matter. At. All.' He made himself breathe. 'Now, come on—the bath's waiting.'

He swept her up in his arms and hugged her against him, their skin-to-skin contact feeling completely natural.

Anna scooped up her hair into a messy knot on top of her head as Jack lowered her into the steaming water. He stepped in behind her, putting his hands on her waist and drawing her backwards between his spread thighs to lean against his chest.

'So decadent, Jack. A lemony bath in a treehouse.'

'They don't have baths in Californian treehouses?' He kissed the vulnerable-looking hollow at the nape of her neck. 'You surprise me. But we need to get rid of this...'

He tried to distract himself with the practical business of unclipping her bra, but the catch was quickly dealt with. He pulled the garment away and dropped it onto the floor, then put his arms around her and rested his chin on her shoulder. He felt her heartbeat quicken as her ribcage expanded into his hands.

He needed to make the time they had perfect, because these memories would have to last him for ever.

CHAPTER NINE

IN A SHADY corner of the deck a wide canvas hammock hung between a post which supported the thatch and a stout branch of the ebony tree. The dizzying drop into the gorge on three sides of the treehouse kept it safe from predators. The only access was up the wooden steps and through the solid door, the way they'd come when they'd taken refuge from the storm the previous day.

An afternoon breeze stirred the leaves against a rinsed cloudless sky. It was almost impossible to believe that twenty-four hours earlier that expanse of blue had been filled with roiling black clouds and riven by lightning. The storm had abated in the early hours of the morning, and with the dawn calm had emerged from the maelstrom of rain, thunder and lightning. The only reminder of the tempest was the gurgle of streams, dry for months, now tipping over the edge of the ravine to plunge into the river. Far below, the watercourse still raged, the torrent of muddy water overflowing its banks, carrying ripped-up trees and other victims of nature's fury on the long journey to the sea.

Anna stretched out a leg and nudged the wooden rail with her toes, setting the hammock into gentle motion again. She lay in the crook of Jack's arm while his fingers twined through her hair. Her linen robe slipped open and she relished the feel of the warm air brushing her skin. She wondered if contentment could be any deeper or the sense of place any more complete.

'Jack?'

'Mmm...?'

His response rumbled in his chest and she placed her palm on his sternum, loving the feel of the hot silk of his skin beneath her hand. He wore a pair of shorts, low on his hips, and she trailed her fingers, barely touching him, down his body to the edge of the waistband.

'Hey.'

'Hey, what?'

'Any more of that and I won't be responsible for what happens next. I don't think sex in a hammock is a safe or sensible idea, but...'

'I never cared much about safety...'

She looked up at him. Grey eyes regarded her from under dropped lids. He inclined his head to brush his mouth across her temple. Her hand flattened against his abdomen.

'Anna...' His chest rose on a rough inhalation. He slid his fingers from her hair and curled them over her hand, lifting it back up to his chest, then pulled the robe across her.

'What happened to the hammock at Themba?' she asked. 'You said it had broken.'

'You remember that?'

'Most of the details of my life at Themba are engraved on my memory, Jack.'

He tucked her in closer against his side. She half turned, placing a bent knee across his thighs. The hammock tilted and swayed.

'Do you remember how excited you always were to come home for the holidays?'

'Of course. I lived for the holidays…for being back at Themba. Back with you…'

'That last time when you flung yourself into my arms for your usual welcome home hug I simply wanted to keep on holding you. But you were innocent and naïve and I couldn't bear the thought of spoiling that. I never wanted you to change.' He smoothed the cool linen over her hips. 'I really didn't want to mess up, and I was trying to limit my exposure to temptation. So I made the hammock disappear.'

'I made it difficult for you. I hadn't a clue what I was doing.'

'Your girlish attempts at flirtation almost drove me wild.'

'And now? Now I'm grown up?'

'Now? You're clever and skilled and incredibly… sexy.'

He paused and she felt his chest rise on a big breath.

'Have there been many…?'

She bit her lip, wondering how to answer him. She'd had lovers, but she'd never loved any of them. And none of her experiences had come anywhere close to what she'd felt in Jack's arms last night and this morning. Again and again he had taken her to peaks of passion and fulfilment beyond what she'd dreamed possible.

'Many lovers? Hmm… A few, but it's never felt like this.'

'How *does* this feel?'

It was difficult to describe. Thrilling? Satiating? Passionate? There were no words to express her depth of feeling, the sense of rightness that permeated deep into her soul.

'Complete,' she said, the word escaping her lips before she could stop it. 'It feels complete.'

'Do you mean it was inevitable?'

'Not at all. This…' she kissed him just beneath the collarbone '…is not what I came back for. But it's happened…'

Anna twisted round and looked out over the ravine, down to the river and the wild land beyond it, keeping her expression hidden from Jack. She didn't want this precious time to be spoiled by questions and confessions. She wanted it to be perfect and…complete. When it was over she wanted to look back on it without regret and without wishing she'd done anything differently.

'Why *did* you come back?'

His question took her by surprise. 'The institute asked me to. You know that.'

'Couldn't they have found someone else?'

'The professor they appointed had an accident and broke his ankle. He should probably never have been riding an e-scooter. If the report had been delayed any longer your application would have missed the deadline and you'd have had to wait another year.'

'And you wanted to help?'

'I was simply doing my job. I'd planned to return one day, and this seemed like a good opportunity.'

Anna tried to keep her tone light. He didn't need to know that she'd thought the short notice meant there'd be no time for her to overthink things and pull out. She'd imagined returning to Themba countless times. Imagined showing Jack just how much she'd grown and achieved, and how little she'd ever really needed him. Her teenage crush had dissolved very quickly, she'd imply, from a cool, professional distance. She'd moved on, formulated a plan for the life she wanted—which didn't include Themba or Jack.

But her careful plan had been derailed. How had she gone from the cool academic who'd stepped off that helicopter to the woman whose wild love-making had made her come apart in his arms last night? She'd never realised how much Africa held her in thrall, or how soul-shatteringly emotional returning to Themba would be. As for seeing Jack again... From the moment she'd set eyes on his tall silhouette at the top of the steps last week she'd known she'd massively under-calculated the misgivings which had surfaced during her journey. That teenage crush had vanished, for sure, but proper grown-up lust had replaced it.

'I've always been curious to explore who I am, and I thought seeing Themba from an adult perspective would help me come to a degree of acceptance about my past. Perhaps it's time to move on from that.'

'And that's what you do? Move on?'

'So far, yes.'

'From relationships?

'Mmm...'

'So if you've never given your heart to anyone you've never had it broken.'

Anna remembered the searing agony of his rejection. How she'd begged him to let her stay with him and his cruel dismissal. He might have been protecting her from his father's clients but it had felt utterly personal and belittling, and she never intended to feel that way again. It might only have been a teenage crush, but having it destroyed had torn her heart to shreds.

Just once, she wanted to say, *eleven years ago.*

But she shook her head. 'No,' she said. He hadn't just broken her heart. Something broken could be mended. He'd destroyed it. 'Never. How about you?'

'Nothing has changed for me, Anna. Themba is all I need.'

'And this?' Her question was soft. She put a hand against his cheek and turned his face towards her. 'Don't you need this? Sometimes?'

'This,' he said, stroking his thumb across her bottom lip, evading the question, 'is something I'm enjoying, very much.'

Anna watched his eyes darken as she took his thumb into her mouth and sucked it.

'God, Anna,' he muttered, 'everything about you drives me crazy. I can't believe this is you I'm holding in my arms. I don't know you any more. At all.'

She let his thumb slide out of her mouth and gripped his hand in her fist.

'I hoped I'd know more about myself after coming back, and I do. Only I'm not who I thought I was. I'd woven a stupidly romantic and idealistic narrative around my parents...' She felt the pressure of his cheek against her hair. 'But now I know my father was a criminal, dealing in illegal blood diamonds, and my mother... How did she come to be with him?' She looked up at him. 'How, Jack?'

He shook his head. 'There's no way of knowing.

She must have loved…him… Hasn't George shed any light on the past?'

Anna nodded against his shoulder. 'He's been able to tell me about my mother. They worked together on research projects. She was a hugely admired doctor, respected in the field of tropical diseases, and she treated rare illnesses successfully. But she gave up everything for love. My father Aidan was a patient. A year after he recovered and returned to Africa she followed him, with no idea of what life with him would be like. She walked away from her career, and her family disowned her in fury and disappointment. But obviously her love for my father overrode all that. It's not something I understand.'

'Mmm… I know it took my father a while to unravel the mystery of that crash,' said Jack. 'They were flying under the radar in every sense. But the names that came up were Aidan Jones and Rebecca Kendall—as you know.' He stroked a finger across her cheek. 'They weren't married.'

Anna nodded, running her thumb across his knuckles. 'My mother wrote to George to tell him about me and asked him to look after me if anything happened to them. He couldn't become my legal guardian because there were no wills, no birth certificate. All official documents had been destroyed.'

'She must have known life with your father would be unpredictable and dangerous. Writing to George meant she cared about what would happen to you if things went wrong.'

'I'd like to believe she cared…'

'She cared enough to choose George.'

Anna felt Jack's arm tighten around her shoulders.

'I remember the day he arrived at Themba to check up on your well-being, when you were five. I was terrified you were going to be taken away.'

'Were you?' She squeezed his hand. George told me he was happy knowing I was growing up in Africa, as my mother had wanted, as long as I got an education. And he also told me it was my mother's wish for me to go to university in England.'

'He must be wise and generous. It could have been so different. And if I'd lost you…'

Anna felt his body tense beside her.

'During those years I felt like you were my whole reason for living. And even though he couldn't be your official guardian, he's been kind to you?'

'He's the kindest, most thoughtful person. I was frightened when I landed at Heathrow that winter, knowing nobody. He did his best to make things easier.'

'I'm sorry, Anna.'

'Some days I felt as if I couldn't breathe in the cold under those leaden skies.'

She waited for him to say it had been hard for

him, too. That he'd lain awake at night longing for her.

But he pulled her into his side in silence, his arm banding around her shoulders, then eased himself on top of her, parting the edges of the linen robe. He dropped his head, resting his forehead against her shoulder. She felt his body stir.

'You said sex in a hammock was unsafe…'

He raised his head, his lips seeking hers, and then he smiled against her mouth. 'If you keep very, very still…'

Her fingers drifted down his spine.

He took a ragged breath and arched his back.

'Not happening, Jackson.'

Pearly light was beginning to sift through the mosquito netting when Jack woke. He slanted a look down at Anna, where she slept curled against him, her back to his chest, an arm crooked under her cheek. If he obeyed the demands of his body he'd wake her gently and make love to her again before the sun rose. But a feeling of unease made him shift away from her and roll onto his back. She stirred in her sleep before her breathing settled into its rhythmic pattern again.

Jack raised himself up on one elbow and watched her. During the past two nights, and some of the day in between, the ecstasy he'd found with her had gone soul-deep. Her responses to him were generous and passionate, and she'd given him more than he had ever expected in his wildest imaginings. In return, he'd broken his own unwritten rule and given her all of himself.

Now, if he laid a hand on her thigh or dropped a kiss on her temple, he knew she'd wake and turn to him, opening her arms. But something held him back.

It had taken only two brief nights for the sight of her in his bed to become one he wanted to hold on to for ever. Two nights for their bodies to become perfectly attuned to each other.

It was the one thing he'd sworn he'd never want.

It was terribly dangerous.

Last evening on the radio Dan had confirmed what Jack already knew. The level of the river was falling. The causeway would be clear by the morning and they'd be able to go back.

He should be pleased, because without his finger on the pulse of Themba he felt untethered and uncertain. He needed to make sure everything was fine, even though Dan had assured him, several times, that there were no problems. For the past eleven years Themba had been his reason to be. His drive and willpower had shaped it into the place it was today, and the idea that it could operate without him, even in a crisis, rattled him.

But, gazing down at Anna's sleeping form, he found the thought of wrenching them from this remote place, insulated from the world, was impossible. It was inconceivable that tomorrow she'd walk out of his life again and this time it would probably be for ever. The perfect life she'd set her heart on wasn't ever going to be here, in the bush and dust of Themba with him. It couldn't be. Because nothing about him was perfect.

Finally, with a jolt that stopped the breath in his throat, he identified the source of his disquiet. During the night, as she'd clung to him, she'd whispered something.

'Jack, don't let me go. Please don't let me go.'

Was she going to wake in a few minutes and beg him to marry her again? Ask him to let her stay?

He sat up and swung his feet to the floor. Grabbing a towel to tuck around his hips, he walked through the door they'd left open so they could make love in the soft night breeze and moved across the deck to lean on the railing.

Anxiety crawled up his spine as he watched the sky lighten in the east. He had to stop this from happening. But he knew it was too late. He'd found the answer to the question he'd asked himself. *This* was how it felt to make love to someone he really cared about and who cared about him.

All the times he'd convinced himself that she was his responsibility, that he had to keep her safe, he had simply been avoiding the scary truth. He'd been too afraid to acknowledge it, but now it was here, staring him in the face, and he had nowhere to hide any more.

He loved Anna.

He'd loved her when she'd emerged from a bundled blanket with her shock of white-gold curls and mesmerising eyes.

But this love was something entirely different.

And tomorrow he would summon the helicopter and send her away again, even though it would rip his heart apart. Even though at her most vulnerable, having given everything of herself to him, she'd asked him not to let her go.

He had everything he wanted and needed here, under his control. Nothing happened that he didn't know about or approve of. The risks he took were calculated. There were few shocks or surprises he didn't anticipate.

He'd learned long ago that he couldn't protect those he loved, and he had no intention of having that proved to him again. Love was more dangerous than anything he'd ever had to face, because losing it left pain that couldn't be controlled. He'd first learned that when his mother had died. Loving someone meant losing control of your emotions, your body, your *soul*.

A tide of fear rose through him at the thought. 'Jack?'

He turned slowly, keeping his white-knuckle grip on the rail. Anna stood in the doorway, her hair messy, the flush of sleep on her cheeks. She had pulled on his spare shirt, which he'd retrieved from the Land Rover yesterday. The sleeves were rolled up to her wrists and the hem hung down to mid-thigh. She was the sexiest thing he'd ever seen.

'Jack?' she repeated, pushing her hands through her tousled curls. 'Come back to bed. It's early.'

She took a couple of steps towards him. He fought for an expression of indifference and she faltered, uncertainty flickering in her eyes.

'Jack, is something wrong?'

He pushed himself upright, looking away from her, down into the valley, where morning mist wreathed the river.

'The river has dropped. I need to get back. There're things to do...'

He saw the hurt flash across her face before she lifted her chin and wiped her expression. His heart lurched.

'Can't they wait a few more hours? Or has everything gone wrong in your absence?'

'No. But I don't like being away. You know that.'

'If that's how you feel I'm sorry we made the trip at all.' She shifted from one foot to the other, obviously confused. 'I thought you were enjoying being with me, but perhaps it was a bad idea in the end.'

Jack shrugged. 'We had sex. Great sex. Now I need to get on with running Themba and you need to get on with finding your perfect life.'

It was as if someone had hurled a brick at her stomach. Anna gasped. She felt her heart crushed in a tight fist of hurt, and with every cruel, cold word it squeezed tighter. How could he be like this after the exquisite tenderness, the sweet words they'd shared just a few hours before?

She fought for breath, trying to push her numbed brain into finding some logical reason for his behaviour. Could this be the same Jack who had cradled her so tightly against him, his arms around her like bands of iron but his lips and hands achingly gentle?

'Is that all it was to you, Jack?' she finally managed to ask. 'Sex? Okay, *great* sex. Thanks for that.' Her voice rose as panic welled up inside her. 'Because it actually felt like something different. To me it didn't feel like we were just having sex. It felt like we were making love.'

She gulped in a breath. All her instincts for self-preservation, which had been dangerously dormant, surged back. She would not let him see how much he'd hurt her and the only thing she could hide behind was anger.

'But obviously,' she flung at him, 'I misread the signals. *Massively.*'

* * *

Jack hardened his expression as he looked across the space which divided them. The look she gave him was level, and then she turned on her heel and walked away.

'We'll leave in half an hour,' he said to her retreating back.

'Fine.' She spun round and took two steps towards him. 'Only I don't think that's long enough for me to say what you need to hear.'

She folded her arms and the shirt—*his* shirt—rose a little higher up her thighs. Her eyes, blurred with sleep a moment before, were suddenly wide, flashing angry green fire. As she advanced across the deck towards him her cheeks glowed, but no longer with the flush of sleep. Anger blazed across her face.

'There's nothing to be said, Anna.'

Jack held up a hand, intending to stop her, but she ignored it. She didn't stop until she was an arm's length from him. He could reach for her, pull her against his body, bury his face in her hair. But he knew that would be perilous.

'*You* may have nothing to say, Jack.' She pointed a finger at his chest. 'But I have enough for both of us.'

Jack gripped the rail behind him with both hands. This was Anna as he'd never seen her, and he had no idea what to do.

* * *

Anna had seen the shutters come down over Jack's face when she'd stepped onto the deck. But she wasn't going to let him off the hook again. It was time he realised she was older, experienced and she didn't need him any more. Most of all, he couldn't manipulate her. *No one* could.

'You're not doing this to me, Jack. Not again.' Her voice shook with fury.

'Doing what? You need to calm down...'

'You know exactly what you're doing—only this time I know, too. And don't patronise me.'

'I don't know what you mean, Anna. All I said was that I need to get back.'

'The *hell* you don't know what I mean... But I'll explain anyway. I've been kind to you, Jack. Patient. I understand why you have a problem with emotions. Awful things have happened in your life. But you've fought for what you wanted and got it—mostly. And that's admirable.'

She took a deep breath and pushed her hair off her face with the back of her hand.

'What's not so admirable, however, is believing you can treat me like you did last time. Haven't you learnt *anything* in the past eleven years? Or even the past *week*?'

The words caught in her throat and she swallowed, suddenly feeling horribly close to tears. But if there was one thing she would never, ever do again, it was cry in front of him.

'Don't cry, Anna, please...'

'I'm not crying. And even if I were, why would it matter? You've decided to shut me out, so why would you care? Last night I went to sleep in your arms. This morning I think it was reasonable for me to expect to wake up in them—not to find you out here, stony-faced, telling me we have to leave before the sun has barely risen. How dare you? How *dare* you behave like this?'

'I... Last night, Anna, you said...'

'Ahh... So *that's* it.' She nodded. 'Well, forgive me for saying something in the heat of the moment, after sex, when I might not have been in perfect control. I don't recall *you* exercising much control last night, either. Perhaps I was thinking back to an earlier time when I actually *wanted* to stay with you.'

'It's...' He pulled his hands down over his face. 'It's... I need to protect you, Anna.'

She shook her head. 'No, Jack, you don't. What you need is to control me—like you control everything else. Losing control makes you panic, and I think over the past week something has... slipped from your grasp. And the only way you can see to get it back is to get me out of your life.'

She looked beyond him, across to the craggy cliffs where the sunrise was steadily shrinking the shadows.

'I've loved being back here, and I'll cherish

these memories, but I'm leaving, Jack—in my own time. And, believe me, this time it *is* what I want.'

She took a step back, afraid that his nearness would shake her resolve.

'There's no reason for me to stay. You've made that very clear.'

Her eyes met his and she saw stubborn anger in their grey depths. He didn't like what she'd said, and he was going to like her next words even less.

'All this time I don't think you've been protecting me at all. You've been protecting yourself.'

Anna turned and walked away from him, anger keeping her head high and her limbs moving.

CHAPTER TEN

ANNA WRAPPED BOTH her hands around the grab handle as Jack accelerated through a section of flooded track. The vehicle lurched as a wheel hit a pothole hidden beneath the water. She twisted her head to look at him.

His frown of grim concentration had deepened. He engaged a low gear and the engine growled as the wheels dug into the mud. His fingers curled around the steering wheel in a white-knuckle grip.

Anna pressed her face to the window beside her and squeezed her eyes shut.

You will not cry.

Returning to Themba had been a huge mistake. It had taken a week—okay, make that about five seconds—for her to fall under Jack's spell again. Or rather for her to recognise that his spell had never been broken. Those years spent searching for the perfect conventional life had been a total waste of time. All she wanted—all she'd *ever* wanted—was right here.

The suburban house with a tiled roof and a neat garden where children could play in safety could all go to hell—along with the boring husband with a nine-to-five job she'd conjured up for herself. She wanted Themba—*and Jack*. Because the two were inseparable. And she wanted all the danger and raw wildness that came with both of them.

But he absolutely did not want her.

She had to do something to distract herself, so she pulled her uncharged phone from the side pocket of the door and plugged it into the lead Jack kept connected in the central console.

'I'll need my phone to make travel plans as soon as we reach the lodge.'

Her teeth had begun to chatter, and she clenched her jaw to hide the symptoms of shock. Then, to disguise her shaking hands, she gripped the seatbelt that crossed her chest.

His face was devoid of expression. 'As you wish. The helicopter is doing a run bringing in supplies this afternoon. I'll see if they can fit you in on the way back.'

'Actually, it'll have to be tomorrow. I've thought of a couple of points I need to verify at the research centre.'

With desperate determination Jack focussed his attention on the road. He risked a sideways glance at Anna, but her face was turned away. Anger at the things she'd said flared inside him again.

As he powered the Land Rover, too fast, down the final slope towards the causeway in front of the lodge Anna's phone pinged. In a reflexive movement his eyes flicked sideways to where it lay between them.

The message was from someone called Brett, and the words he saw included 'beach' and 'with you'.

His foot hit the brake and the wheels locked in a violent slither of mud and gravel. He hauled on the steering wheel to correct the skid, realising with a shock that he'd been close to losing control again.

And not just of the car.

Anna released one hand and snatched up her phone. 'Be careful or we'll land upside down in the river, Jack.'

He was damned if he was going to apologise.

So that was why she'd been so keen to charge her phone. She'd been waiting for a message from *Brett.* Whoever he was, he hated him already. Was he a contender for providing Anna's perfect forever home? The two-point-four children?

Fuelled by an anger intense enough to scare him, he accelerated across the low bridge at a dangerous speed and the big vehicle bounced as it hit the cattle grid.

He knew he'd been looking for a hook to hang

his behaviour on, and now he pretended he'd found it. There was another man in her life. Probably some slick blond Californian. That explained her even honey-coloured suntan, some of which, he suspected, had been acquired topless. There was someone else who kissed her, held her, made her scream like he'd done.

It was an unbearable thought.

He punched the brake and swung the Land Rover to a gravel-biting stop at the foot of the granite steps. Before the quiet settled around them Anna had released her seatbelt and had her hand on the doorhandle. Jack eased the stranglehold he had on the wheel and flexed his aching fingers. He stared straight ahead, through the filthy windscreen.

'Who the hell,' he grated, unable to help himself, 'is *Brett*?'

Anna's feet hit the ground and she whirled round to face him. Some icebergs must be green, he thought distractedly. He was sure they were the exact colour of her eyes now as they bored into his.

'He's a…a friend. In California.' She began to turn away. 'Not that it has anything at all to do with you. Open the rear door, please, so I can get my backpack.'

Jack didn't mean her to hear his next remark, but he mistimed it. 'A friend with benefits?'

'Yeah. *Great* benefits.' She slammed the door.

* * *

Anna dropped the backpack on the slate floor of her suite and doubled over, pressing her forearms into her abdomen. Real pain clawed at her, and she thought she might be sick or pass out. She tried to breathe rather than gasp, but the tight band around her chest made it almost impossible.

After a minute she found her way to the armchair. Pulling her knees up to her chest, she curled into a ball and released the scorching tears that she'd been aching to shed for hours.

How had she not realised this visit was a terrible idea? She should have known it was a fast-track route to heartbreak. *Renewed* heartbreak. Dismissing her feelings for Jack as a teenage crush had simply been an attempt to protect her pride and restore her own self-confidence.

Now, with the dubious advantage of experience and maturity, she faced the stark truth. Nothing and no one could ever replace Jack in her heart, but he had no space in his life for her. He'd told her that truth eleven years ago and nothing had changed except the fact they'd had sex. Mind-blowing, incredible sex, which she'd stupidly thought meant something more than simply satisfying their own desires.

Her body shuddered with the sobs which rose from somewhere so deep inside her she couldn't believe they'd ever stop. It frightened her to be so out of control, at the mercy of such raw, destructive emotion. She pushed her knuckles into her mouth and bit on them, hoping if she concentrated on the pain she'd be able to bring her panic under control.

It felt like hours before the crying began to subside and the tears slowed. She scrubbed at her eyes with the backs of her hands and then stumbled to the bathroom to splash cold water on her face. Her throat ached and her eyes burned.

Bracing herself against the hard edge of the handbasin, she stared at her reflection in the mirror. She looked a total mess, but she was beyond caring. What mattered was that she'd *allowed* this to happen. And as she peeled off her clothes and stepped under the shower, she vowed she would never, ever expose herself to such vulnerability again.

With her washed and dried hair bound in its neat braid, some make-up applied and dressed in jeans, white shirt and jacket, layer by layer Anna restored her outward professional appearance. Her carry-on bag took only moments to pack, and then she sat cross-legged on the floor and wrote a note on a sheet of the Themba stationery.

She placed the folded paper under the heart-shaped pebble on the coffee table. When Jack had given it to her he'd promised that every time she held it she would know he was thinking of her.

She had no plans to hold it ever again.

As she picked up the phone to speak to Reception she heard the approaching beat of the helicopter...

Jack turned from his office window as Dan came into the room. He kept his hands bunched in his pockets because they still shook with anger. He couldn't switch off the sound of Anna's voice, and the more he thought about what she'd said, the angrier he felt. He had to get his thoughts in order—and then he'd confront her and tell her just how wrong she was about him.

'You okay, Jack?' Dan sounded uncertain.

Jack unclenched his jaw. 'I'm fine.' He faced Dan across the desk but did not sit down. 'Tell me what I need to know.'

Dan shrugged. 'Not a lot. Everything's okay. We were more worried about you and Dr Kendall than about anything here.'

Jack frowned and rolled his shoulders. 'Nothing happened to us. The treehouse was a good suggestion.' A sense of disbelief coloured his next words. 'Are you sure nothing went wrong while I was away? It was a ferocious storm.'

'There was some damage to the perimeter fence. We've repaired it and checked the rest of the boundary for weak spots. Mud washed into the swimming pool, but we've sorted that.'

'Anything else?'

'The power went down for a few hours, but the generators kicked in on cue, so that wasn't a problem.'

'Is that all?'

'Pretty much, Jack. We coped.'

Jack realised he didn't want to hear that. It made him feel superfluous, a little aimless, and his anger deepened.

'Right,' he bit out. 'That's good. I'll see you later.'

He threw a belated 'thank you' at Dan's back as the other man left the room.

He had to see Anna now. Make her listen to him and understand his point of view. His childhood experiences meant that her safety had become his prime concern. For her to suggest he'd always had his own interests at heart was ungrateful and cruel, and he was going to tell her exactly how wrong she was. It was the only way he could defuse this rage.

He followed Dan out of the office, slamming the door behind him.

She wasn't at the research centre, and when there was no answer to his knock at her suite he tried the door.

'Anna?' He stopped in the middle of the room, glancing towards the bathroom. 'Anna...?'

He slid back the glass doors and scanned the deck and the bush beyond the rail. He went back inside and his eyes fell on a folded sheet of thick Themba writing paper on the coffee table, weighed down by a stone in a shape he recognised.

His stomach dropped as realisation hit him and panic detonated in his chest.

The room was empty, and not just of Anna and her possessions. Her essence, which had enveloped him ever since she'd arrived, had gone with her.

The space where she'd been felt more than empty. It felt desolate and abandoned. And what hurt so much that he gasped was that she'd left behind that little pebble, and all it meant.

Jack sat on the edge of the armchair and picked it up, closing his fingers around the cool stone. Then he spread the paper out on the glass tabletop. She'd gone, she said, on her own terms, in her own time. Could he, she asked—and there was cool politeness in every neat, cursive word—dispose of the diamonds and make sure the people who'd found her after the accident benefited in some way from the proceeds? And, lastly, would he please not contact her? Ever.

He smoothed a finger around the edge of the little heart, rubbing it with his thumb as if he could magic Anna back like a genie from a lamp, so he could explain to her why he'd had to make her leave. Why they could never be together. She made him lose control, and he couldn't live with that because it terrified him. His mouth dried and his stomach lurched at the thought.

But she'd gone. For good. And her manner of leaving had demonstrated, if he needed to be shown, that he no longer held any sway over her. He knew his behaviour had shattered and hurt her, but she hadn't collapsed or crumbled. Her strength of will and confidence shocked him once more.

He glanced at his watch and a spark of desperate hope fired in his brain. There might still be time to stop her, so he could explain…

But as he stepped outside he heard the accelerating throb of the helicopter and saw it lift into the air beyond the trees. It dipped to the left before levelling out and heading south, diminishing with every second until it disappeared into the afternoon haze. His heart echoed its beat long after he could no longer hear it.

Jack tried to breathe. Anna was gone and she'd never come back. He'd never hold her again, feel her hair beneath his cheek or hear the little sound she made when he kissed her. He'd lost the most precious thing in the world and he was entirely to blame. The only person he could direct his anger towards now was himself.

CHAPTER ELEVEN

GEORGE WAS SEATED at his favourite table in the corner. Anna knew he liked admiring the gardens from the shelter of the Orangery Restaurant, and so he'd have his back to her as she approached.

She threaded her way through the restaurant, slipping out of her jacket and shaking her hair free of her beanie hat. Summer had given way to early autumn during the time she'd been back in London, and the leaves of the trees in Kensington Gardens were gilded with gold.

'George!'

He turned and his face cracked into a wide smile. He stood and drew her into a hug and then kept his hands on her shoulders for a little longer than usual. When he'd kissed her on both cheeks and taken her jacket and bag to dump on a spare chair, she was aware of his close scrutiny. She'd learned early on in their relationship that while he might appear laid back and lost in thought a lot of the time, not much escaped his keen notice.

She was fine with that. She didn't intend to

hide anything from him. But she didn't plan to tell all, either.

When they'd ordered their food and drinks, and she'd stopped arranging her bag, checking her messages, tucking her phone away and basically exhausted her supply of delaying tactics, George propped his folded arms on the table and leaned in towards her.

'So, Anna. Tell me all about it.'

Anna met his penetrating blue gaze, slightly magnified by his black-rimmed glasses, and dropped her eyes to her hands, where they tangled together on the starched tablecloth.

'Where do you want me to start? The job? The trip? I'm negotiating terms for the job, but...'

'Oh, the job...' He waved an expressive hand. 'The job can wait. I want to hear about the trip.' He inclined his head. 'It must have been emotional, going back.'

Anna talked her way through her serving of crisp fish and chips, and George listened as he ate his poached salmon, nodding occasionally, sipping from his glass of wine.

'I'm pleased to see you eating well,' he remarked, as Anna picked up a chip with her fingers and dipped it in ketchup. 'You look a little thin. Or is that the result of a couple of months of Californian clean eating?'

'Mmm... Maybe.' The truth was she hadn't eaten much since she'd left Themba. Everything tasted like sawdust and eating was way too much trouble.

George's arched eyebrow expressed his scepticism. 'Have you submitted your report?'

'Yes, last week. They asked for a meeting. There were a few points that needed clarification.'

'Such as?'

'Oh. Um… Questions about my previous connection to Themba and how much I'd interacted with…the team.'

George signalled to the waiter and requested coffee, glancing at Anna for confirmation. Then he looked out at the gardens. A breeze had picked up and it rustled through the trees, bringing a flurry of leaves drifting to the ground.

'You've told me the *work* story, Anna,' he said. 'Now tell me the story of the shadows in those green eyes. What really happened?'

Anna shifted on her chair. Their coffees arrived and she stirred hers for longer than necessary before sipping it while it was still too hot. She sat back and released a long breath.

'I thought I could use the visit to find out more about my parents. I wanted to feel some kind of connection to them. I hoped I might get a sense of who I really am, now that I'm an adult and able to ask the right questions.'

'And that didn't happen?'

'Well, yes… And then no. At first I was excited. J-Jack showed me some clothes he'd found after I left. The ones I was wearing when the plane crashed. Dungarees and a tee shirt with an elephant...' She shook her head. 'Sorry, George, you don't need to know this. It's boring for you.'

'Not at all. I'm really very interested. Go on.' He kept his eyes on her face as he raised his coffee cup.

'Seeing—*touching* the clothes was...surreal. The thought that my mother had dressed me in them, on that last day... It was the closest I've ever felt to her. But then Jack showed me a stash of uncut diamonds that had been sewn into the pockets. That was shocking.'

George's expression sharpened. 'Ah. So things got a bit complicated.'

'Well, yes. It seems, from rumour and supposition, that my parents were smuggling diamonds when their plane crashed. It explains why there was no record of the flight, no destination logged.' She shrugged. 'Suddenly my whole existence felt...*tainted*. The romantic vision I'd created of my parents was utterly wrong.'

'I'm sorry Anna. That must have been extremely upsetting. But, you know, even though it ended in tragedy, their story *was* a romantic one.' George gripped his hands together and rested them on the table.

Anna stared into her now cold coffee. George summoned the waiter and asked for a fresh cup for her. She bit her lip. Then she looked at him again.

'I get that it was a romantic story. You've always impressed that on me. But I don't understand... I just *don't*.' She shrugged. 'My mother was intelligent, highly qualified, respected. How did she fall in love with someone who was nothing more than a criminal, dealing in blood diamonds, whose dishonesty and greed ultimately killed them both and almost killed me?' She shook her head. 'Whoever I am, I'm half of that person.'

'Is that it? What's bothering you?'

'Oh, that's not the end of the story. Jack took me to the site of the crash, to meet the people who rescued me. I thought I'd feel something incredible at the place where they died, where I'd last been with them, but I didn't. I felt empty and pointless. I just wanted to leave. And then I think Jack felt sorry for me. And...'

George scrunched up his napkin in a fist and then released it onto the table. He sipped from his water glass.

'Anna.' He leaned forward again. 'There's something I need to tell you. I've had news from Themba.'

CHAPTER TWELVE

JACK TOLD HIMSELF he'd soon feel better. He'd coped without her before. He'd do it again. But her final words hammered in his skull, tormenting him, and as the days passed and his anger cooled, allowing him space for rational thought, he began to believe she was right.

When she was eighteen he'd sent her away earlier than necessary. It was true that he'd been protecting her from his father's guests, but his far greater fear was that if she stayed any longer he'd lose control of his emotions, leaving him open to renewed pain and loss when she left to study in England.

He'd had his emotions in an iron grip for most of his life. His mother's death, dealing with his father, losing Anna...all had taught him how to maintain it. Only Anna had come close to breaking it. He would never let that happen—could never take the risk of loving again.

He'd poured all his energy, all his passion, into improving and running Themba, making it the place he wanted it to be and the place where he wanted to be—because that was where he felt safe. *In control.*

Had he always been simply protecting himself? He resented the fact that Anna had left without giving him the chance to refute her words and explain his motivation. That he'd never have the opportunity to do it was driving him crazy.

And then he received a message, via a complicated chain of communications. The elderly man who had been part of the group they'd met at the crash site wanted to see him again.

Telling Dan he'd be out of touch for a few days, he headed north, following the route he and Anna had taken two and a half weeks before.

His relief at escaping the place where everything—*everything*—now reminded him of her did not last. The route was littered with memories of their trip: the place where she'd exclaimed over a bossy family of warthogs, trotting across the road, the particularly rough bit of track where she'd hung on with both hands, her laugh of delight as he'd slammed on the brakes, allowing a tortoise to complete its stately amble across the track in safety.

And the place where they'd stopped and he'd told her about his father's death.

Wherever he could, Jack floored the accelerator, determined not to linger over either the memories or the places. He knew he was driving recklessly, but it kept his mind focussed on the present, not mired somewhere in the regret of the past, or untethered in the bleak, shapeless future.

When he arrived, the old man invited Jack to sit in the sun in front of his home and offered him sweet bush tea. Then he bent and pulled what looked like a metal strongbox from under his chair. It was battered, scorched, and the lock had been forced.

'I should have given this to you the day you came with the girl.' He pushed it across the earth towards Jack.

'I have been afraid of it for many years and hid it from my sight. But that day I saw you are a good man. You tried to help her. And at the mine they say you are fair. That you care for your workers.' He nodded towards the box. 'You will know what to do.'

Jack bent forwards, fingering the broken catch and padlock. 'Where did you get this?'

His host shrugged. 'You can see it is damaged and burnt, as if from an accident.'

The hinges were rusted, and they creaked as Jack prised the lid open. He sucked in a quick breath of shock. No wonder it was heavy. It was filled to the brim with rough diamonds. He ran his fingers over them and then raised his eyes to meet the old man's calm gaze.

'What do you think I should do with it?'

The man sipped from his mug of tea. 'Whatever is right. We heard that they were involved in…bad things…illegal diamond dealing.' He glanced at the box. 'After I found it I did not know who I should tell. Nobody came to investigate the crash for many months. It was as if the plane, and the people in it, had brought bad magic. Everyone feared it. I was afraid for the child, so we took her away to Themba, where she would be safe. And I buried the box. I did not want it to be mine because I knew it would bring trouble, but I did not want to pass on trouble to anyone else.'

Jack picked up one of the pearly lumps of rock. 'So why have you changed your mind?'

'Ah…' He smiled. 'This will not bring trouble to you, because you will know what to do. Also, I wish to die in peace. I do not want my spirit disturbed by an old tin in the ground.'

'Do you expect to die soon?'

Their eyes met over the rims of their mugs.

'Who knows? But it is best to be prepared.'

Jack propped his elbows on the railing of the tree-house deck and cupped his chin in his hands. Stubble scraped his palms. It felt as if he'd been on the road for a week, but it had been only three days.

He could have headed straight back to Themba, but he'd needed the headspace and the silence in which to explore and confront himself, and now he knew what he would do.

He had something that would make Anna very happy, but he had to do more than that for her. He needed to show her how he meant to change and how he wanted to at least try and allow himself to love her. She might reject him—he wouldn't blame her for a second if she did—but he had this one shot at true happiness and fulfilment and he had to stop trying to protect himself from hurt and go for it.

The thought scared the hell out of him, but the idea of not trying, of never knowing, scared him more.

The irony was that the old man had thought the diamonds were the valuable part of the box, but he'd been wrong. Because half an hour ago, when Jack had tipped its dusty contents onto the deck, he'd found something far more precious underneath them.

CHAPTER THIRTEEN

ANNA'S FINGERS GRIPPED her coffee cup, her shoulders rigid.

'*You've* heard from Themba?' Cold foreboding rolled through her. 'Why? What's happened?' She shook her head, feeling confused. 'I haven't heard anything... Is it Jack? Has he...? Has there been an accident?'

Images of the lion crouching on the track, the elephant charging Jack's father, the huge crocodile near the causeway, all flashed across her mind.

George reached out and covered her hands with his. 'I'm sorry. I should have been more specific. I've had news from Jack, to be precise, and he's fine.'

Relief swamped her as the adrenaline rush ebbed. Only George's firm grip kept her hands from shaking. 'Then what...? Why has he contacted you?'

'It's an interesting story, and one which you'll hear in full when the time is right. But the most interesting part of it is this.' George's gaze was unwavering. 'Jack has found your birth certificate.'

'What?' A fresh wave of adrenalin pumped through Anna's veins. She half stood, but George's hand anchored her forearm and pressed her gently down again. 'How is that possible? Where did he find it?'

'All those questions will be answered in good time.'

Anna heard the strain in George's voice, and she thought she saw pain in his eyes. 'What is it, George? What's wrong?'

'Nothing's wrong, but there is something else I need to tell you.' He propped his elbows on the table, tension straining his shoulders. 'Your mother Rebecca and I were research partners. But to me she was more...much more...than that. I loved her deeply, but it wasn't enough. I couldn't compete with Aidan's dashing romanticism.'

'Oh, George...' Anna tried to take a sip of coffee but her hand still shook. The cup rattled against the saucer. 'She broke your heart, and yet you've been amazingly kind to me.' She sniffed. 'You might have resented me.'

'As you know, I was pleased and touched when she wrote to tell me of your birth. And when I finally found you, living happily at Themba, the relief was immense. I've always taken my unofficial guardianship of you seriously, and I'm extremely proud of what you've achieved. How could I possibly resent someone who has brought so much joy to my life?'

Anna attempted a smile, but her lips felt wobbly and wouldn't co-operate. 'Thank you. You've been my rock, George. You always will be. I'd never have achieved any of it without your love and encouragement.'

'Whatever your thoughts about your father, remember that Rebecca loved him enough to give up everything for him. And you must believe that Rebecca loved you very, very much, too.'

Anna nodded. 'I'll try to see it that way, and to believe she loved Aidan.'

'What I remember most about Aidan is his air of fierce determination.' A corner of his mouth lifted in a half-smile. 'I think you inherited that determination from him.'

Anna managed to smile back. 'But when did you hear from Jack?'

'Yesterday. He called me.'

'And he asked you to tell me he'd found my birth certificate?'

'He thought you'd be happy to know it has come to light. But he also said you'd asked him not to contact you, so...'

'That's true. I was angry and hurt... Did he tell you anything else?'

'I think Jack would like to tell you the story

himself, if you'll let him. But perhaps you should tell me about what happened with him first?'

Anna pushed her fingers into her hair and massaged her scalp. 'There's nothing to tell. Not now. I left. I said I didn't want to hear from him. I…'

'Why?'

'I…misread the situation. I thought what we had was something more than…what it was. Jack can't do emotion or love. He does control and management. You know me. I want it all. The house, the husband, the family. The stuff I missed out on.'

Even to her own ears she sounded unconvincing.

'That "stuff", as you call it, is meaningless if there isn't true love and steadfast commitment at the core of it. You were happy at Themba. You loved your life and you didn't want to leave it. How do you know you'd love your version of perfection?'

Anna hesitated, tapping the side of her china cup. 'I don't. I suppose I look at other people's lives and see the stability and consistency I never had and think it's desirable. Some people I met at university had families who'd lived in the same houses for generations. That intrigued me. Because when they asked where I was from, how did it sound when my answer had to be *I don't know*?'

'To them it probably sounded impossibly exotic and romantic,' said George. 'But what about Jack? What does *he* want?'

'Nothing. He wants nothing more than he already has—although when we were…together… it felt as if he wanted…me. But for his own complicated reasons he can't trust himself enough to allow himself to love.'

'Do you love him?'

George's blunt question was a shock. Anna felt tears threatening again and she forced them back.

'Yes. I do.' It was difficult to shape the words. 'Very much. Enough to give up my dreams of the perfect home and husband and family. Enough to make my life with him, whatever that means.'

'Have you told him that?'

'No. Why would I subject myself to another rejection?'

'What if he knew that what he has at Themba is what you want, too?'

But she knew it was too late. She'd walked away without saying goodbye—again. She'd left her precious talisman pebble behind. When he found it he'd know without doubt that she'd wiped him out of her life.

She'd truly burned all her bridges. She'd achieved what she'd set out to accomplish and proved to Jack that she didn't need him.

She'd never let him know the truth.

Picking up her bag and jacket, she stood.

George sat back and watched her. 'Where are you going?'

'Where I always go when I need solace.'

'The Natural History Museum?'

She nodded, then bent to drop a kiss on his cheek. 'I'll let you know what I decide about the job.'

When she turned at the door to wave he was looking at his phone.

Crowds swarmed along the pavement below, but there was only one face Jack was looking for. His heart thumped against his ribs as a lithe figure peeled away and began to run up the shallow steps. Every muscle in his body tensed. Would she pass him without a sideways glance? Would she see him and turn away, refuse to talk to him?

He curled his fingers into his palms, fighting to stay calm.

But Anna stopped three steps below him. Slim blue jeans encased her long, long legs, and a loose-fitting black jumper brushed her thighs. An index finger hooked her jacket over one shoulder. Her hair shimmered, rose-gold, in the soft autumn sunshine.

He wanted to tell her he preferred her hair loose, and wanted to close the distance between them and ease his fingers into that French plait and tease it out, so that he could bury his face in the matchless silky ripple of it. But he stood and stared, drinking in her image, feeling his tired body fire up with all kinds of need.

'Jack?'

She climbed another two steps towards him and he caught her perfume on the air, saw her knuckles turn white around the strap of her bag.

'Anna.'

'*Jack?* How on earth…?' She shook her head. 'You're supposed to be at Themba.'

'I was—yesterday morning.'

She mounted the final step and he caught her in his arms, breathing her in, wanting every inch of her against his body. Her heartbeat was as loud as his own and just as quick. He slid his fingers to the nape of her neck and pushed them into her hair, tipping her face up.

'I just want to look at you.'

He pressed his forehead to hers and then, unable to resist her, dropped his lips to her mouth. She tasted sweeter than in all his memories, and pure, hot desire mainlined around his body. He shifted his thighs, slid a hand down her spine and clamped her against him, feeling her mouth driving him frantic.

But her response was to press her palms against his chest and push him away. With her forest-dark eyes, her lips rosy from kissing and her flushed cheeks, she was more beautiful than he remembered. He tried to pull her back in, but she resisted.

'No.' Her breathless voice was throaty. 'I'm not doing this.' She shook her head. 'I can't.'

Anna leaned against the cushions in the corner of her sofa as Jack sat down in the chair opposite. They'd walked in silence through the South Kensington streets, and she'd led him to her flat because she needed to be in a place where she felt in control and safe.

She cradled a mug of tea in her hands, tucked up her feet and studied him. His grey eyes, dark as a storm cloud, ranged over her. The lines etched between his straight brows deepened as he placed his own mug on the table between them.

'What are you doing here, Jack?'

His eyes interrupted their tour of her body and returned to her face. 'I'm here now, but I've been to all nine circles of hell since you left.'

It was an unexpected response. She felt uncertain of his mood.

'I needed to get away and you wanted me gone.' She sipped her tea. 'You were quite clear about that.'

'Yeah, but that doesn't mean it wasn't hard as hell. I thought I'd never see you again.'

'And that bothered you?'

'More than I could ever express. But I needed time to think, to work things out. I hadn't realised how difficult that would be when everything... everything reminded me of you.'

Anna put down her mug and gripped the end of her plait in her fingers. 'What things have you worked out?'

He took a few moments to reply. 'I've decided to step back. I want to appoint Dan as general manager of Themba, freeing me to concentrate on conservation and development. I'll oversee the extending and commissioning of the research centre and the school and find new staff.'

'My report...'

Jack held up a hand. 'Wait. If I...*we*...don't get the funding, I'll sell some shares in the mine. While I'd like the recognition the institute can give us, finances won't be a problem.'

'Are you sure you can do this?' Anna watched his face. 'Giving up total control of Themba and the mine are two massive steps.'

Jack pulled a hand over the back of his neck. 'No. I'm not at all sure. I like—I *need*—to be in control. That's no secret. Handing over to someone else, however capable they are, will be hugely difficult. But I've got a great team and I need to cut them some slack. Start trusting them. I believe it's the best way forward for Themba. Ultimately my plan is to turn it into a co-operative, but I haven't worked out the details yet.'

'Have you discussed this plan with your team? Or is it something you're going to implement without their input?'

'Not yet. But obviously—okay, *not* obviously,

given my track record—I *will* listen to their opinions. I have to get myself out of the middle of things. God, Anna, after you left I had to find space to *think*. I haven't done that... I haven't *allowed* myself that...since I don't know when. So when I got a message from the old man who found you, it was the opportunity I needed to get away.'

Anxiety fluttered in Anna's stomach and she threaded her plait through her fingers. 'Did *he* have my birth certificate?'

'In a way, yes.'

'I...I had lunch with George today. In Kensington Gardens.He told me you'd found it.'

Jack nodded. 'I know.'

'You *know*? How?'

The corners of Jack's mouth lifted in the ghost of a smile. 'George told me where to find you, obviously.'

'You were waiting to hear from him?'

'Mmm...' Jack reached into an inside pocket of his jacket and pulled out a brown envelope and a folded piece of paper. He held the paper out to Anna.

Anna's fingers trembled as she unfolded the document. 'I'd given up hope of ever seeing this.' She looked up at Jack, finding his gaze steady. 'It feels odd. As if I now have a proper beginning on which to build the rest of my life. I didn't *want* my father to be a crook, but George has made me realise how much my mother loved him. I want to respect that.' She reached out to take the envelope from Jack's hand. Two battered passports slid onto her lap, followed by a faded photograph of a young couple. The man stared at the camera and Anna could see the blaze of determination in his eyes. The woman's soft gaze was turned to the baby she held in her lap. Tears blurred Anna's vision. 'Thank you, Jack.' She wiped tears from her cheeks. 'For as long as I can remember I've wished for a photograph of my parents. In a way, with this and my birth certificate, I feel as if I can start afresh.'

'In California?'

'Perhaps.' Anna put the documents on the coffee table but kept the photograph in her hands 'Now, you've described your plan for Themba. But what about you?'

'What about me? I'll be working harder than ever. Conservation is the ethos at the heart of what Themba stands for, and that's what I'm passionate about. I'll be able to make a bigger difference if I don't have to spend time entertaining ecologists and professors. Dan's very good at that side of things and he loves it.'

'What you mean is you'll be setting yourself impossible standards and continuing to beat yourself up about things over which you have no control.'

'Anna, every time poachers kill a rhino or an

elephant I have failed in my duty of protection. I can work to prevent that.'

'For over two decades you've blamed yourself for your mother's death, then you added your father's to that burden of guilt. You've made yourself responsible for every living thing, animal and human, on Themba land, and that's amazing. But you can't keep them all safe, Jack. Stuff happens. Sometimes it's bad stuff. It might happen less, but it'll happen, and if you isolate yourself…if you won't allow anyone to support you through the bad times and rejoice with you in the good ones…you're going to…'

'Drive myself crazy. Yeah. So that's why I'm here.' Jack leaned forward and propped his elbows on his knees, pushing the heels of his hands into his eyes. 'I loved my mother. And my father. In different ways.'

He pulled his hands away and his look was so bleak it cracked her heart. 'Jack, I…'

'It may shock you that I loved my father, in spite of how he was. But I loved the man he had been…and the one he should have been.'

Anna's stomach clenched. When she'd lain in Jack's arms she'd allowed herself to imagine that he might love her, but he'd dashed that thought with a few words. She tried to steady herself before she spoke again.

'But Jack…' She took a deep breath, steeling herself. 'When you and I… What we felt…'

'When you asked me not to let you go, I re-alised something that terrified me. I couldn't let you stay even if I wanted to.'

'*Why*, Jack?'

'What if I asked you to stay, but you left me? Life at Themba isn't what you want. What if I ended up losing you, too?'

Anna wrapped her arms around her shins, wanting to put out a hand and comfort him but afraid she'd drive him further away.

'It wasn't your fault, Jack,' she whispered. 'You were eight years old. None of it was your fault.'

He looked at her as if he didn't understand. 'My love has never been enough. I'm afraid it never will be.' He stood up and walked to the window, keeping his back to her. 'But, Anna, I have to try. Because I've realised that the worst possible thing would be not at least *trying* to love you. All those years when I took care of you, pro-tected you, had you in my life, it wasn't respon-sibility I felt. It was love. I've loved you from the first moment I set eyes on that little girl with the platinum curls and emerald eyes, wrapped in a blanket. For years our friendship was inno-cent, and I hated it when it changed. I wanted it to always be the same. But I couldn't deny that I wanted you. I tried. God, I tried. I had to get rid of the hammock. I had to force myself to stop hugging you when you came home from school. When I made you leave it wasn't only because I couldn't protect you from the predatory men my father insisted on entertaining. It was to protect you from me.' He dropped his head. 'You had to go to London. It was your mother's wish. But if I'd let you stay another three days, never mind three weeks, I'd have given in to your naïve attempts at seduction. It was all I wanted to do. But it would have been absolutely wrong.'

Anna stood and followed Jack to the window. She wrapped her arms around his waist and laid her cheek against his shoulder blades. Tears burned in her eyes.

'I don't need to be protected from you, Jack. All I need is for you to love me.'

He went very still. When he spoke his voice was quiet. 'Themba is unbearable without you, Anna.' He turned in her arms and took her hands in his. 'Everything—absolutely everything—reminds me of you. I buried our memories for years, but when you came back I found they were all there, in bright Technicolor, haunting me every moment of the day and most of the night. And now there are new ones. But the life I lead isn't the life you want. I know that.'

Anna raised a hand and stroked his cheek, longing to feel the roughness of his unshaven skin against her body instead of just her palm. She placed a finger on his lips.

'I planned to prove I didn't need you, but I hadn't counted on my heart telling me that I always will.' She pressed her forehead against his chest, breathing in the scent that was just uniquely…*his*…and kissed the knuckles of the hand which gripped hers. She raised her chin to look at him. 'My mother had a successful career as a specialist in tropical diseases, but she gave it all up to follow Aidan to Africa, to an uncertain life full of challenges and danger. She gave it all up for *love*, Jack, because love was—*is*—more important than all the material trappings in the world. And it turns out I'm very like my mother. Your love means more to me than all my dreams of a conventional life. All the things I thought would make me happy would be meaningless without you.'

She turned her cheek into the warm cotton of his shirt, listening to his heartbeat and to his breath hitch in his chest.

'Africa is my birthplace, Themba is where I grew up, and I love them both. I think you know that. But most of all I love you, Jack, with every fibre of my being and with all my heart and soul. I've always loved you. I want to share in the tough times and help you celebrate the successes. I want to care for you as you have always cared for me. I want to help you to love me.'

She couldn't wait another second to taste his mouth again, so she slipped a hand round the back of his neck and buried her fingers in his thick hair, pulling his head down until their lips met.

Jack's powerful arms encircled her, sealing her against his hard body as his mouth and tongue plundered hers. He groaned, cupping the back of her head in one hand while the other traced a path down her spine, making her arch into him.

When he tore his mouth away and rested his cheek on her hair they both gasped for air, their hands entwining again.

'Anna, I've dreamed of this—of having you in my arms, in my bed and in my heart—but the fear of losing you has stopped me from believing it could ever happen. I might drive you insane with my over-protectiveness while I get used to it.'

Anna smiled up at him. 'I'm strong and tough, Jack. You made me that way, teaching me how to live in a place like Themba. I think I can tolerate anything—even your over-protectiveness—if it means being loved by you. Together we'll be stronger than we could ever be apart.'

Jack's mouth took hers in another long, deep kiss. He slid his fingers to the nape of her neck, where she felt them nudging into her hair, loosening her plait. So she tugged at the ribbon and teased the strands free.

'That's better,' he murmured.

She felt the brush of his mouth on the top of her head. Then he lifted her off her feet and cradled her against his chest, his lips feathering across her temple.

'I'm never, ever, letting you go again, Anna.

You're the missing piece that completes me. With you I feel strong enough to face my fears.'

He carried her over to the sofa and eased himself down, settling her across his lap.

'We'll build a new house at Themba. Dan can move into the huts. If he'd like to.'

Anna frowned. 'As long as it has a thatched roof and a deck with a hammock, I'm in.'

Jack pushed a hand into a pocket of his chinos and withdrew it with his fist clenched. 'You left something behind, Anna. Hold out your hand.'

Anna flattened her palm and felt Jack release the cool, familiar shape of the pebble into it. Hot tears brimmed in her eyes. 'I told myself I no longer wanted it, but I missed it so much. Almost as much as I missed you...'

Later, as darkness crept across the windows, Anna lay in the crook of Jack's arm, her fingers entwined with his.

'So the diamonds that were sewn into my pockets were just the beginning? There were far more of them?'

He nodded. 'I think those in your clothes were the ones that wouldn't fit into the box. It was crammed with them. If I hadn't tipped them out I would never have found what was underneath them.'

'What will you do with them?'

'We can add them to the ones we already have

and then they can be analysed. We can probably discover where they originated. That means certificates can be issued for them and they can be legitimately sold. And since the people who found you also technically found the diamonds, the proceeds can go to them. I think our elderly friend will see to it that the money is carefully spent for the benefit of everyone in the village. He's anxious to leave a good legacy and to be untroubled in the afterlife.'

'That's what I'd like to happen, if possible.'

'Are you sure? You could keep the proceeds yourself, you know. How about a cottage in the country? A really fancy watch? Or…?'

Anna turned and punched him gently in the ribs. 'Stop it. You know that's not what I want.'

'Oh? Would *this* be more to your liking?'

He smoothed the palm of his hand over her hip. She turned her head into his shoulder.

Jack's eyes darkened as her body began to thrum under his long, exploring fingers. Her breathing stuttered when his mouth found the super-sensitive place under her collarbone. She loved that he'd remembered it.

Holding her gaze, he lifted a lock of hair from her forehead and stroked it behind the curve of her ear. 'I love you, Anna. I *need* you. Please say you'll stay with me for ever.'

As her focus narrowed, and her awareness contracted until it was concentrated solely on the man she loved, Anna curled her fingers around his hard biceps.

'That, Jack, will be the realisation of my wildest dream.'

EPILOGUE

ANNA AND JACK were married in a ceremony on the deck as the summer heat softened and the shadows grew long. The wedding celebrations began immediately afterwards in the boma—a traditional, circular enclosure of thorn branches around a fire pit. It was a new addition to Themba, built in three months for the wedding, and the new events manager had plans to make it available for other exclusive celebrations, offering guests a taste of Themba hospitality alongside the opportunity to engage with the latest conservation initiatives.

A log cracked and a column of sparks wreathed in smoke hissed upwards into the night sky. The insistent beat of traditional drums swelled, growing louder and quicker, underpinning the ululating chant of the women who swirled and clapped, bare feet stamping in the dust.

Firelight flickered over the hundred guests who had gathered to witness the marriage and celebrate far into the night. Every branch held a sparkling lantern, and garlands of fairy lights were looped through the trees and across the tables where dinner had been served.

Anna and Jack could hear the festivities from where they stood under the ancient baobab tree in a corner of the compound. The graves of Jack's parents had been tidied and planted with indigenous flowers, and a headstone had been erected to mark them.

Anna knelt to place her wedding bouquet beneath it. Jack drew her to her feet, clasping her hands to his chest and running his thumb over the square-cut emerald ring and the gold wedding band on her finger.

'Thank you,' he murmured, pulling her against him. 'Since I allowed myself to love you and to accept your love in return I've been able to remember my parents with love instead of with anger and guilt. For the first time I feel they're at peace.'

Anna reached up to kiss him. 'We'll always remember them, Jack.' She squeezed his hands. 'I promise.'

The celebrations had reached fever-pitch and a great cheer went up as they appeared in the arched opening in the stockade. Anna's oyster silk vintage dress, embellished with a delicate tracery of pearls and jewels, gleamed in the firelight, her hair rippling over her shoulders from beneath a wreath of cream roses.

As they paused Anna's gaze travelled over the assembled guests and tears pricked her eyes at the number of familiar beloved faces she recognised.

George, who had walked her across the deck, kissed her cheek and then placed her hand in Jack's, smiled, his eyes bright.

Brett, who had come all the way from California, took a brief moment out of the sensuous dance he was enjoying with her bridesmaid Emma to blow her a kiss.

Emma, an old school friend, had flown up from Cape Town, where she worked in the university's Oceanography department.

Dan, whose awesome organisation skills had solved every problem in the lead-up to this day, lifted a hand in a half-salute.

Joseph, who'd given her invaluable bushcraft lessons, had come out of retirement to see them married.

And two colleagues from the institute, who had arrived with the news that Jack's application had been successful, were engaged in a furiously energetic drumming lesson.

Jack slid an arm around her waist and bent his head.

'How many of these buttons are there, Anna?' His fingers traced a heated path down her spine. 'And how long is it going to take me to undo them?'

His hand came to rest in the small of her back.

Anna slanted a look up at him. 'As long as you don't rip them off...'

Her breath caught as his slow smile sent heat racing through her.

'Not promising, Anna,' he murmured, 'but perhaps it's time to go and make a start?'

Accompanied by a surging tide of well-wishers, they made their way on lamplit paths to where the Range Rover waited. As they rattled over the cattle grid and crossed the causeway Anna looked back at the cheering crowd. The sight of the boma, glowing in a halo of golden light under the starry sky, and the fading sounds of drumming and singing raised goosebumps across her skin.

She reached out to rest a hand on Jack's thigh. 'I think the party's just beginning,' she said.

The glance he threw her was intense. 'You bet.'

It was after midnight when they reached the Ebony Tree Lodge. The steps were strewn with summer bush flowers and a bunch of aromatic herbs had been fixed to the door. Jack put an arm around Anna's shoulders and the other behind her knees and swept her up. He shouldered the door open and carried her through the treehouse onto the deck.

The feel of the voluptuous silk moving over her skin as he let her slide down his body almost shredded his control. His hands cupped her face and his thumbs brushed her cheekbones. The moonlight filtering through the leaves bathed everything in a wash of silver, but her eyes, holding his, shone like the emerald on her finger.

'Anna...'

'Mmm...?'

His mouth dropped to take hers in a gentle kiss, but then she made that sound in her throat that drove him wild. The grip he'd been forced to exercise on his desire since he'd turned and seen her on George's arm, walking towards him across the deck, finally slipped.

As their kiss soared out of control, he slid a hand to the back of her neck and began to undo the little silk-covered buttons...one by one.

* * * * *